THE OVERBOARD MISTAKE

A MCLAUGHLIN SISTERS NOVEL (STRANDED IN GETAWAY BAY ROMANCE, BOOK 2)

ELANA JOHNSON

*I*ris McLaughlin tapped something on the huge desk calendar in front of her. "And don't forget to get over to Henry's," she said, glancing up at Amelia. "He's twice a week in this heat."

"Twice a week," Amelia deadpanned, because Iris had told her all of this before. Maybe she was a little nervous about leaving the success of her business in someone else's hands.

She'd built We'll Weed That from the ground up, literally. The company had started with her weeding a few people's yards in her time after school back in her teens. She'd incorporated once she'd graduated, and she moved on to complete lawn care. Mowing, weeding, fertilizing, trimming.

A few years later, she'd hired two landscape architects, and her business in Getaway Bay had taken off. She hadn't changed the name, and now We'll Weed

That had a full-scale nursery, as well as unique yard designs to go with their landscaping upkeep.

"Where are Sam and Betty?" she asked, deciding she didn't need to go through the list with Amelia. She looked down the hall as if her general manager and her lead construction guru would appear simply because she wanted them to.

"Probably kissing just outside the back door," Amelia said, her eyes sparkling now.

Iris giggled, though it probably was true. She didn't want to go on this cruise with the happiest couple on earth, but they'd earned the prize. Never mind that she hadn't been out with anyone in eight months and that her sister had just gotten engaged to a billionaire.

Wouldn't that be nice? she thought dryly, though she didn't want to get stuck on Bald Mountain Bluffs for a couple of days the way Eden had. But she would take the handsome boyfriend with loads of money.

Her daydreams continued, only interrupted when Betty came down the hall with her duffle bag over her shoulder. "Are you coming? We've been outside waiting for you for twenty minutes."

Had it been that long? Iris tended to run late to almost all of her appointments, no matter how early she left. "Coming," she said, tapping the end of her pen on the countertop before ducking into her office to grab her bag.

The three of them drove across Getaway Bay to the dock where the fourteen-day cruise disembarked.

They'd go around all the Hawaiian islands, and out toward a group of islands that could only be seen in certain times of the year. Apparently, the beginning of March was a great time to see whales, dolphins, and the sometimes submerged islands, and every email she'd gotten about her cruise had indicated it would be packed full of people.

Iris rode in the back of the company vehicle, her nerves twittering just a little bit. When they arrived at the office, Betty threw her a scathing look and said, "We need to hurry, or they'll give our tickets away."

"They will?"

"You have to check in by ten," Betty said, practically running toward the door. "It's after that already."

Chaos reigned inside the tiny trailer that housed the cruise's office. Iris could barely get inside, and it was clear people wanted to be in here rather than outside because of the misters running and creating a warm, tropical atmosphere.

Betty pressed her way to the counter, and Iris followed her. "Betty Terrace," she said. "Sam Potter. Iris McLaughlin."

The woman there scanned the sheet in front of her, though Iris could clearly see everyone else had checked in. "You barely made it," she said as a bell rang. The crowd started shuffling toward a side door. "That's the bell for the orientation." The woman stamped a piece of paper and started rattling off instructions.

Iris barely listened, because the pull to go with the

other bodies called to her. She waited beside Betty, though, until she said, "Great, thanks," grabbed the papers, and hurried after everyone else.

"I'm sorry," Iris said, taking her sheaf of papers from Betty. "I didn't realize what time it was." How much time had she lost romanticizing things in her head? Too much. She always did.

Betty smiled at her, though her eyes were still a bit hooked, and slid onto the second to last seat in the back row. Sam sat beside her, and Iris glanced around for another seat. People truly filled the room, and a blip of anxiety flowed through her when she realized this really was a fully-booked cruise. The room probably held fifty people—and the only seat remained was up front, next to a man who was so wide he practically filled both seats.

Iris went that way, because the man at the front of the room was watching her, clearly waiting for her to sit before he began. She'd never been as grateful for her petite frame as she was when she slid in beside the tattooed military man.

His hair reminded her of dark roast coffee, and his tan skin testified that he spent plenty of time out in the Hawaiian sun. He flicked his black-as-coal eyes in her direction, and she tried a smile on her face.

Surprisingly, his lips twitched upward in return, and Iris focused on what the man up front was saying. "This is a great time for whale-watching," he said. "And there's a pod of humpbacks that have been seen every day for the past couple of weeks." He glanced around with a huge smile on his face. "We should see those later today. We'll dock tonight at Maui, but we won't be getting off. We leave port in the middle of the night to sail around the island to Lanai. We will disembark in Maui on the way back."

Blah blah blah. Iris had seen the map of the cruise. She knew where she was going and when the boat would stop and where she could get off. She relaxed now that she was here, the cares and worries of her landscaping business somewhere in her past.

"Our last stop is north of the Hawaiian island chain, at a group of islands that are rumored to convert even the most unlucky in love."

Iris perked up then. This line of mystery islands intrigued her, and she couldn't wait until day nine, when their ship would arrive at them.

"Several people got marooned there in the seventies," the man continued. "And five couples ended up getting married by the pilot who happened to be a priest."

"That's so romantic," Iris sighed, wishing they could get off and explore the island.

The guy next to her that was practically sitting in her lap scoffed, and Iris's eyes flew to him. "You don't think it's romantic?" she whispered.

His dark eyes sparkled like dangerous stars. "No," he muttered. "It's not even true."

"How do you know?"

"I served in the military," he said, as if his precise haircut, folded arms, and hint of his dog tag necklace didn't already tell her all of that. And what did him serving in the military have to do with the islands? Maybe he was Coast Guard, but he looked more like a Marine to her, especially with those tattoos.

The man up front went on to talk about things that were left behind when the couples got rescued, and how the islands were submerged in the fall and early winter when the rains came.

"So buddy up," he said. "You don't have to share rooms, but we want to make sure everyone has someone else on the cruise accountable for them."

Iris felt like she'd been transported back to fifth grade, when teams were being picked for kickball. Not particularly athletic, she never got chosen until the very end. Eden, her older sister, was the athletic one. The one teaching everyone about outdoor survival, the one who knew exactly how to hike, where to look for food, all of it.

She glanced around, noticing that people had already paired up around her.

Everyone but the tattooed meathead who didn't have a romantic bone in his body.

"I guess it's me and you," he said. He didn't look happy about the pairing at all.

"I guess," she said, still looking around. If Ivy were here, she'd know exactly how to charm this guy. But her twin had literally gotten all the flirting and talking genes, and Iris just stood there like she'd lost her ability to speak.

"Now that we're ready," the man said into the microphone. "Check in with your buddy, and let's get on the ship."

It seemed like all forty-eight other people under the tent moved as a single unit, and Iris accepted the fact that she'd have to report to this Marine from time to time over the next fourteen days.

"I'm Iris McLaughlin," she said as they joined the line to check in and board.

"Justin Brunner," he said, and even his name sounded angry.

Iris sighed, trying to make it a quiet one. She didn't succeed as Justin looked at her with raised eyebrows. "You're not looking forward to the cruise?"

"No, I am." Betty and Sam had disappeared, and the vacation she'd been dreaming of vanished right before her eyes. "You?"

"No," he said. "This isn't really my scene."

"Why are you here then?" And alone too. Of course, she was alone as well. Sort of.

"Work," he said, stepping forward.

"Is that all I get? Work?" Iris wasn't sure where the sass had come from. He certainly wasn't the type of man to appreciate sarcasm, and the glare he gave her solidified that.

"I'm developing an app for this cruise line," he said

coolly, handing the woman his ticket and adding, "Iris McLaughlin and I are partners."

"Welcome to Cruise Hawaii," the woman said with the fakest smile on the planet. Justin smiled back, but it also radiated more of a chill than anything else.

Iris handed her ticket to the woman, got the same spiel, and headed for the boat, once again the last one to make it up the walkway to the boat.

Her nerves attacked, and her feet froze before she got on the ship. *Go on*, she told herself, especially when Justin turned back, an inquisitive look on his face.

The boat horn sounded, and she was going to get left behind if she didn't get on the ship right now.

"Come on," Justin said, sudden compassion in his eyes. He reached for her, and she put her hand in his as a woman on the dock yelled at her to go.

Her skin tingled as Justin all but hauled her onto the boat, the gangplank got removed, and the vessel lurched away from the dock. Her legs trembled, and she lurched, falling right into Justin, who certainly had the arms to catch her.

CHAPTER TWO

Justin could not believe he'd been saddled with the one female on the cruise that required special assistance. It was as if he'd attracted women like Iris McLaughlin. To many giggles and not enough substance.

Maybe it was the tattoos.

Or maybe there had only been one seat left in the audience, he told himself as he steadied her in his arms. "Have you been on a cruise before?" he asked.

"Not really," she said.

"That was a yes or no question."

"No," she said, stepping back and brushing something invisible from her blouse. She wasn't dressed properly for a cruise either. Who wore heels and a pencil skirt to sail around for fourteen days?

"Why now?"

"I always reward my top two employees of the

year," she said. "This year, they wanted to take this cruise."

"And you came with them?"

"Yes," she said, something guarded in her voice. Justin wanted to know what it was as much as he convinced himself he didn't care. Just because he and Iris were "buddies" didn't mean they actually had to spend any time together.

"Okay, well, I'm going to go find my room," he said, lifting his bag. "I'm sure I'll see you later." The ship was a decent size, and there were only fifty people on board. He'd definitely be seeing her later, and he wasn't sure if he was excited about that or dreading the moment.

The Web Developer had paid for him to have a premium room on the main level of the boat. He went down a hall, away from the pool and restaurant and turned left before finding his room. It did seem quiet enough, though Justin had brought earplugs and knew how to use them.

He couldn't believe he'd agreed to come on this trip. He could build an app for a company without experiencing every step someone might take, but for some reason, Theo had really wanted him to have "the full experience."

Maybe because his last two blind dates Theo had set up for him had ended in disaster. Maybe this was his boss's way of punishing him further. Justin shook his head as he tried to get his keycard to work. The light stayed stubbornly red, and while he'd spent many years in the Navy and then as a SEAL, his patience for this day was almost out, and it wasn't even noon yet.

Someone else approached, and he nearly dropped his card when he saw Iris. "Your room is right there?" She shook her head, a smile curving those pretty lips. "Figures."

Before he could ask what that meant, she swiped her card, got the green light, and went inside her room. The door slamming closed felt like a very final punctuation mark on their conversation for the day, and Justin went back to trying to get inside his own room.

In the end, he had to hunt someone down and get his keycard reset. Only then could he get in the tiny room with the even tinier bed. This was almost as bad as sleeping in bunks on a submarine, and he'd done that for a while too.

He could do this. It was sitting by the pool and eating as much as he wanted. There was a gym here, and he could lift weights in the morning the way he always did. He made a few quick notes for the app—*have a way to call someone to a room in case a guest couldn't get in, as well as the ability to add a buddy to a profile before the guests even showed up.*

Then, he wouldn't have been surprised by the cute little blonde next to him. She hadn't wanted to be his partner, he could tell. He hadn't spent two and a half years in Navy SEAL training to be oblivious. He could read people easier than most, and he hated that he now knew every way off this ship from the location of his room.

He knew where the lifeboats were, and how many, and how much weight they could handle. The SEAL in him hadn't died just because he'd retired last year.

A year ago this week, in fact, though Justin tried not to think about it. He'd gotten a good job, with a good company, and the Navy had paid for his college education years ago. He'd been stationed with the SEAL team in Pearl Harbor for the past five years, and he had no complaints about that either.

In fact, his biggest complaint about Getaway Bay and his life here was the boredom. The most exciting thing that had happened to him in the year since he'd retired was building over twenty feet of a path that had fallen in a landslide last summer.

The construction. The working with people again. The rescue. All of it had brought a part of him to life that he'd thought dead. He couldn't go back to the SEALs, and he didn't really want to. But he'd been thinking about changing jobs, getting out from behind the cubicle walls, and doing something else.

What, he didn't know.

And his attempts at dating had been worse than his attempts at finding another job. He'd never put much stock in marriage and family while he was with the SEALs. He'd seen too many lives torn apart when loved ones in the military didn't come home. He hadn't wanted to put anyone through that.

But now that he was retired, he was extremely lonely. He wanted to share his life with someone.

The pretty blonde next door?

He scoffed out loud at the thought. No. But someone.

His shoulders barely fit on the bed, but it would do. He'd slept in much worse places, that was for sure. He didn't think there was anything about the room that needed the app—maybe the ability to call for housekeeping or report something broken. He made a mental note of it and exited his room.

Iris seemed to have tuned right into his frequency, because she came out of her room before his spring-powered door could close. She held a white and yellow towel and had pulled all that blonde hair up into a ponytail.

"Going to the pool?" he asked, and she spun toward him.

A smile bloomed on her face, and despite himself, Justin smiled back. "Yes," she said. "Apparently there's karaoke later tonight."

"How did you know that?" he asked.

"There's a whole entertainment guide in the room," she said. "You didn't see it?"

Justin hadn't looked for it, so he simply said, "Nope."

"I'm a terrible singer, but I figure I might as well have fun while I'm out here. You know?"

That was an attitude Justin could get behind, and he

said, "Good plan," and gestured for her to go ahead of him down the hall. He hadn't changed or grabbed a towel from his room, but he figured the pool and bar area of the ship would be as good a place as any to waste some time.

That was what this whole cruise was. A waste of time. His time. Theo's time. The company's time. But they'd paid for the whole thing, and Justin knew this Cruise Hawaii line wasn't cheap.

He had a meeting with the owner on Day Ten, when they looped back around Maui on their way back to Getaway Bay. He hoped he'd have something intelligent to recommend by then, and he added the entertainment schedule to the list of things that should definitely be accessible via the app.

The atmosphere at the pool was party-like, and Justin scanned the crowd, realizing he was definitely one of the oldest people there. How he'd missed this fact in the trailer and then under the tent, he wasn't sure. At thirty-eight, he wasn't Jurassic by any means, but most of the people here looked to be in their twenties and early thirties. Early-early thirties.

One little old couple lay in a pair of loungers across from him, and they didn't seem to notice the game of chicken being played by two women in the exact same red bikini a mere five feet from them. Maybe they usually wore hearing aids and had taken them out. That was what Justin would've done.

In fact, he reached into his pocket and pulled out

his phone to turn down his hearing aids. He'd gotten them, courtesy of the Navy, a few years ago after a mission where he'd lost most of his hearing in a bombing overseas.

That done, he noted that the pool was too small. He didn't have to put that on the app, but it was simply good to remember for his own personal comfort over the course of the next two weeks.

He turned to the bar and ordered a soda with mango syrup in it. Theo had bribed him onto this boat with the promise of all the sugary drinks he could get. If Justin had a weakness it was mango Diet Mountain Dew, and the first sip relaxed him.

He was glad something did, because the sight of Iris easing out of her swimming suit coverup to reveal a one-strap garment was enough to send his pulse right back into the stratosphere.

Maybe he did like her. Maybe he'd try to set up his own date for once. He kept his eyes on her as she lotioned-up her bare shoulder, running her fingers deliciously close to the top of her suit.

His throat felt like sand, and he quenched his thirst with his soda. But it was the wrong kind of thirst in his gut, and his fantasies moved through him with the power of gravity.

Iris lifted her eyes to his, and Justin glanced away. But he'd been caught staring, and he knew it. Though he stood in the shade, everything felt too hot, especially the weight of Iris's eyes on him.

He steadfastly refused to look at her again, and eventually, another woman came to get something to drink. She smiled at him too, but she'd already been cuddling with another man.

Taking a chance, he looked back to where Iris had been. Her bare legs stretched in front of her on the lounger, and she had her nose buried in a book.

She was gorgeous, Justin could admit that. So maybe he could put up with a little giggling.

Maybe.

THAT NIGHT, HE WAS AWAKE WHEN THE SHIP pulled out of Maui. Sleeping on a boat wasn't as easy as people thought, and he hadn't been the only one to go to the only all-night food bar to get something to eat around midnight.

He hadn't seen Iris there, or again since he'd finished his soda and high-tailed it back to his room. He hadn't come out for any entertainment, and he was taking that knowledge to the grave. Theo had texted to ask him how the cruise was so far, and Justin really hated that he was so accessible all the time.

The ship lurched, throwing him off the bed in his room. Concern ran through him in waves, but he'd been in plenty of military operations that had startling things happen. This was a cruise ship, and while its maximum capacity was only fifty and it wasn't huge, Justin didn't think anything serious would happen.

Cruise Hawaii had been in business for fifty years. Everything was fine.

Until he got thrown against the wall, the slim desk pressing into his stomach. He glanced down at the entertainment guide, truly concerned now.

And when the red light started flashing above the door in his room, the situation moved to a whole new level.

*I*ris jolted awake when someone banged on her door. The red, strobing light in her room struck fear right behind her breastbone, as did the voice that said, "Iris. Get up. It's Justin."

Justin.

She'd seen the man watching her as she got ready beside the pool. The next time she'd looked, he'd been gone. She hadn't seen him at dinner or karaoke, and she'd commanded herself to stop thinking about him.

He wasn't the only handsome man on the ship. Maybe the only *available* handsome man, as this cruise seemed to be full of couples in their mid-twenties. But she wasn't going to hook up with him for two weeks and then go back to her real life. No, she wanted a man that *became* her real life, and she didn't think he was up for that.

Bang, bang, bang. "Iris."

She threw the covers off her legs and took the three steps to the door, pulling it open before he could pound on it again. "What's going on?" The lights in the hall continued to flash, alternating red and white flashes.

"We've got to get to the lifeboats."

"What?" she asked. Or she tried to. The ship heaved again, throwing her to the left and into her doorjamb while Justin skidded a foot or two down the hall.

"Something's going on with the ship," he said.

"I need to change," she said, glancing down at her purple silk pj's. These weren't fit to wear out in public, in a lifeboat, or while she waited for a rescue ship.

Her saliva turned to sand as she tried to remember everything Eden had taught in her outdoor survival classes. Thankfully, her sister had packed her an emergency kit, and she ducked back into her room amidst Justin's protests.

She didn't care. She wasn't getting in a lifeboat nearly naked, with no supplies. She pulled her jean shorts over her pj's and grabbed the nearest T-shirt her fingers touched. Ten seconds later, she whipped open the door again, one arm in the T-shirt while the other held her hip pack full of the supplies Eden had deemed necessary for a cruise.

"Ready," she said. She'd taken one step toward his outstretched hand when the ship lurched again, almost like something had hit it. "What is going on?" She stumbled forward, almost losing the battle against gravity.

"Attention, passengers," a voice said, blaring through the speakers overhead. "The ship is sinking. Please make your way to the closest lifeboat and proceed to evacuate."

Justin muttered something under his breath, and Iris couldn't hear him through the panic pounding in her whole body. *Don't let go of his hand,* she told herself over and over. *Don't let go of his hand.*

"This way," he barked, turning left when she would've gone right. They went to the front of the ship, and Justin peered over the railing. The lights illuminated the water, and Iris saw something there.

"What—?" she started at the same time he said, "Killer whales. They're attacking the ship." He bent his knees as if he could tell another blow was coming—and it did. As the ship righted itself, Iris got thrown against the railing. If she hadn't been clutching Justin's hand so tight, she'd have gone right over.

Right into the pod of killer whales below.

She'd seen them before in domesticated shows, and they were beautiful and majestic. Great big animals in black and white, with smiles on their faces.

But this pod was angry for some reason.

"Come on," Justin said, towing her away from the whales while the captain continued to order an evacuation of the ship.

While Justin spoke in a clipped, commanding tone that irritated her she knew he was her only chance of getting off this ship alive. "There's a lifeboat back here."

Just the one, and he put her hand on the railing and looked right into her eyes. "Don't let go, Iris." He set about untying the boat and checking the killer whales, seeming to do everything with exactness in the least amount of time possible.

The splashing over on the left side of the boat lessened, and she thought maybe the whales had decided they'd had their fun. Another lurch told her something different, and Justin said, "Almost got it."

"Why didn't anyone else come this way?" she asked, glancing over her shoulder. Most of the guest rooms were located on the upper decks, and none of them had stairs that came down this side.

"Let's go," Justin said, picking her up as if she weighed nothing and climbing up on the railing.

"Whoa. What are we doing?" Her stomach swooped, and she clung to his shoulders as if her life depended on it. Because it did. And wow, his shoulders were spectacular. Broad and warm and strong.

"We're jumping," he said a moment before he did it, and Iris shrieked as she fell. He held her in one arm and onto a rope with his other hand, easily kicking off the boat as they went down, down, down to the lifeboat.

He set her on the bench, said, "Hold on," and pushed them away from the cruise ship. She had no idea which way they were going. No idea where anyone else was. The most eerie sight she'd ever seen was that brightly lit cruise ship floating away from her, the lights flashing on the small crests of waves the whales made as they continued to nudge it, test it out, and push it where they wanted it to go.

Iris wasn't sure how long she watched the boat, but it couldn't have been more than twenty or thirty seconds.

Then the lights on the ship went out completely. A collective cry went up from everyone still onboard, and it chilled her to her very core.

"Justin," she said as she sucked in a breath. She knew the boat was there. She just couldn't see it, and that was so eerie, the hair on her arms stood up.

"Turn around, sweetheart," he said. "Don't watch it."

She wanted to watch. It was a train wreck she couldn't look away from. But she allowed him to gently guide her so her body faced the other direction. But he couldn't erase the sound of people yelling and calling for help. A shiver ran through her body, and he tucked her under the safety and warmth of his arm.

"In the morning, we'll find somewhere to stay," he said, his voice a mere ghost in the darkness.

Iris wanted to cry, but no tears came. She wanted to ask where in the world he thought they'd stay in the miles of water surrounding them, but the words stayed quiet.

Her fingers unclenched around the strap of her hip

pack. She hastened to put it around her waist, and then she leaned into Justin's strength again, praying for a miracle when morning came.

THE SUN ROSE, PAINTING IRIS'S EYELIDS WITH warm, golden light. She opened her eyes, thinking the ship was rocking more than she'd expected it to.

"Morning, Sunshine," Justin said, and she sat up straight as a gasp came out of her mouth.

Frantic, she glanced around. Only blue, glinting water in every direction.

They were going to die out here.

She hurried to unzip the hip pack, her heart beating a rapid staccato in her chest. The phone felt like security in her hand, but it had no service.

"Mine's out too," Justin said. "We were using the WiFi on the ship."

Iris twisted to look behind her, but there was no sign of the ship. More water. More waves. The thought of a killer whale trying to capsize their boat drifted through her mind, making every muscle tense. "What are we going to do?"

"Well, it's west over there," he said, pointing toward the horizon on his left. "Because the sun is coming up over there. I've been keeping us moving north, because that was where that chain of islands was." He glanced at her. "The ones you thought it would be romantic to get stranded on."

She couldn't tell if he was teasing her or not. Her heart beat so strangely in her chest, but that could've been from the panic. "At least there will be supplies there," she said.

"You think so? From the seventies?" He shook his head. "I don't think so, Iris."

She liked the way he said her name now, when his voice wasn't full of bark and bite. She'd liked it when he'd called her *sweetheart* last night, and *sunshine* a few minutes ago.

"Well, my sister teaches outdoor survival classes," she said. "She packed this hip pack for me. So we have some stuff."

He glanced down at the small pack around her waist. "That thing is tiny."

"It's something," she said, feeling defensive of Eden for some reason.

"I rescued your sister and her boyfriend," Justin said, drawing Iris's attention away from the pack.

"You did?"

"Last year, right? On the Bald Mountain Bluffs trail." He practically puffed out his chest. "I led the expedition to repair the path and get them down. Me, a couple of other retired SEALs, and a team of paramedics."

"You're a Navy SEAL?" No wonder he was ripped from muscle to muscle. And so demanding.

"Retired," he said, glancing away.

"So what do you do now?"

"I develop apps," he said. "I was going to do one for Cruise Hawaii. I'm seriously reconsidering it."

For some reason, his words struck her funny bone, and Iris started laughing. Maybe she'd gone crazy already, out in all that open water. Maybe she was exhausted, though she'd clearly slept a little bit under Justin's arm on the lifeboat.

No matter what, her laughter filled the sky, and she liked the sound of it. "Yeah, I'd seriously reconsider it too," she said. "Or be sure to put in an SOS option for if a pod of killer whales starts to attack the ship."

"Good idea," he said, the twitch of a smile playing along his lips. "And hey, at least we got to see some whales. The humpbacks are the most popular, because they're seen the most. But the killer whales are rare."

"Yeah?" Iris shaded her eyes to look into the rising sun. "Well, I'll be honest and say I'm not sure I'm glad to have seen them."

"No kidding," he said, and Iris gave him another smile. This time, he returned it in full, and wow, he was absolutely breathtaking in the morning sunrise, that grin on his strong mouth, and those dark eyes sparkling as if they knew a secret about her.

Iris wasn't sure how long they drifted on the boat, Justin always keeping them in a northward direction. She thought south would've been better, as that was where the actual chain of Hawaiian islands were, but he'd refused to budge in his command of the oars. So north they went.

He scanned the horizon constantly while they talked. Little things about siblings and jobs over the years. Stuff she'd tell a guy on the first or second date. Except this time, Justin couldn't go anywhere, and she'd have to see him again in the morning.

Probably right here on this boat.

Her stomach turned, and she finally opened her hip pack to see if Eden had put any food inside. She pulled out two packaged squares labeled protein cookies and handed one to Justin.

"Is there water in there?"

Iris rummaged around, though he was right and this thing wasn't very big. "Water filtration kit," she said.

"An umbrella?" He peered down into her lap. "I'm guessing no."

"Did you just make a joke?" She looked at him through her eyelashes, enjoying the sensation of flirting with a handsome man.

"Maybe." He grinned. "But if she's got emergency blankets, we can maybe make a little tent or something to stay out of the sun."

She pulled out a bottle. "Sunscreen." Iris gazed at his tan shoulders, her fantasies flying into high gear as she imagined spreading the lotion over those beauties.

"My eyes are up here," he said, and she jerked her attention back to his face. He laughed, and the sound of it was warm and wonderful, sending sparkles through her whole system.

"Funny," she said, stuffing the sunscreen back into her pack. She dug around a little, trying to get her blush under control, when he said, "There's an island."

He stood up, rocking the boat because of the movement of his weight.

She looked up too. "What? Where?" She couldn't see anything but glinting sunlight on waves.

He pointed straight ahead. "Right there. See how there's a white streak where the waves are crashing against the shore?"

Iris squinted, desperately trying to see it. Justin leaned over and put his hand right alongside her cheek. "Right there."

All at once, she saw the waves he was talking about. Excitement built in her chest. They wouldn't have to stay on this boat forever, hoping a passing cruise ship would find them.

"It's going to be rough going in," he said. "Look at that tide."

Iris had no idea what that meant, but she didn't like the sound of "rough going in."

"Let's get ready," he said. "You got any rope in that pack?"

CHAPTER FOUR

Iris had a length of cord that wouldn't break, but it wasn't a rope. He still had her tie her hand to the side of the boat and kneel down in the middle of it.

Justin balanced his weight right in front of hers and heaved against the oars, trying to get past the break in the ocean. His muscles strained as he tried again and then again, but the heavy waves beat them back every time.

With his shoulders burning, he stopped rowing and let the waves push the boat away from the island.

"What are we going to do?" Iris asked, panic evident in her voice.

"I'm going to get us over the break," he said. "And then the waves will just push us in." He eyed the cliffs to the right, knowing he'd probably need to steer them away from those even over the break.

"How are you so calm?"

"No one's shooting at me," he said, rolling out his shoulders. "What's there to panic about?"

Iris opened her mouth to respond, then shut it again. The hint of purple silk waved to him from underneath the collar of her T-shirt, and Justin looked away. She'd actually been smart to pull her clothes on over her pj's, because now she had more clothes to work with. And he had a feeling they'd need every supply they could get once they made it to the beach.

His stomach cramped from the lack of food, but he'd been through worse. There was nothing as hot and miserable as the Middle Eastern desert, and though he felt fried from being out on the water in the sun for hours, he'd survive.

And no one was shooting, so there was that too.

"All right," he said, rowing parallel to the break now. "I think I'm going to try a bit farther down. It looks a little calmer." He pushed against the waves, glancing over his shoulder to see when the next one was coming. They rowed past it, losing a few feet but gaining several. Pull after pull, he moved them toward the break, a grunt escaping as he put everything he had into the next drag.

"Come. On." He strained against the water, angry with himself for ever finding the ocean beautiful. It certainly wasn't now, not when he wanted it to help him and all it could do was work against him.

The oars came out of the water, and he started

losing precious inches. He dove them right back in, heaving against the weight of the world while his muscles ripped and another groan tore from his mouth.

"You've got it," Iris said. "Don't give up, Justin."

Her cheerleading wasn't entirely necessary, but he liked it just the same. It gave him the drive and the strength to dig into the water one more time, pulling them the last few feet over the break.

Without anything giving him resistance now, he fell forward in the boat as the oars gave way—right onto Iris.

She grunted too, and Justin realized his face loitered only inches from hers. Her eyes were the clearest of blue, and Justin suddenly liked the color of them. Like the ocean.

The waves pushed the boat closer to the beach, and he used that momentum to get himself back up and onto the bench in the middle of the boat. "You can untie your hand," he said, grabbing hold of the oars so they weren't flopping around.

He checked their position, and sure enough, they were drifting toward the cliffs. Of course, the waves wouldn't just guide them right to the white sand beach. But Justin could get them there. He rowed, bringing the boat back to the beach and where it would wash up on the shore.

When the bottom of the boat scraped sand, Justin took his hands off the oars, feeling calluses starting to form there. When he was an active SEAL, his hands would've been hardened and able to row a boat anywhere. Now, since he spent his time in front of a computer, he'd softened.

He jumped out of the boat, the shallow water warm against his legs, and pushed the boat up the shore. "We'll need this, most likely," he said, thinking they could use it for shelter, firewood, or any number of things he didn't know about yet. To fashion a weapon. To get around to another part of the island. The possibilities were endless, and he didn't need the ocean stealing the boat.

After pushing it up several more feet just in case the tide came in while they were exploring, Justin faced the beach in front of him. Palm trees. Banyans. Green, lush-covered land that swelled gently.

And behind him, the constant, never-ending rush of waves rolling in. Justin turned in a circle, searching and scanning for anything that made sense. Beside him, Iris finally got out of the boat, her pink-painted toes sinking into the sand beside him.

"Okay," she said, her voice full of air, carefully concealing her panic.

"Okay," he echoed, wishing his phone worked. He could call Theo, who had more money than he knew what to do with. He'd get a boat out to rescue them, and maybe Justin and Iris would only have to be here for a couple of days.

But his phone was now just a timepiece. "Shelter

first," he said. "Then we work on water. Then food." He started up the beach, expecting her to follow.

"I've got the water purifier," she said from behind him. "Why don't we start there?"

"Because we need somewhere to stay out of the sun," he said. "It's brutal." Sapping his energy, dehydrating him, and making him see things that weren't there.

Like a beautiful woman he wanted to take to dinner. He shook his head and kept walking though Iris wasn't following him. She would. She couldn't survive out here without him.

He reached the tree line and stepped into the blessed shade. Relief hit him, and he refused to let his thoughts focus on anything but the mission at hand. Shelter. Water. Food. It wasn't cold, and if they got the essentials in place, they'd be fine until help came.

What if help doesn't come?

He pushed the thought away, because it didn't do any good to hypothesize on what-ifs. He knew that. Had served enough missions where there'd been enough paths to take. He had to focus on the one right in front of him.

"Iris," he called as he turned. She still hadn't moved from her spot next to the boat. Annoyance flashed through him. And to think he'd thought he was ready to start dating. He'd even installed that singles app that had made Theo a billionaire and had been chatting with a few people.

He approached Iris and schooled his emotions into something as soft as he could. "Hey," he said, stepping beside her. "You've got to get out of the sun. You're red already."

She looked up at him slowly, a glazed look in her eye. Shock. "They won't see us if we go into the trees." She sniffled and wiped her face with one hand.

"They're not coming right now," he said.

"When will they come?"

"In a few days," he said. "I'm sure the boat radioed back that they were having trouble, and the cruise line will send a new boat. But that's a day and a half. Two days." Justin had no idea if what he said was true or not. He didn't even know if the boat had been sunk.

But he didn't think so. If so, where were all the other lifeboats?

He said nothing, because he didn't want Iris to know he may have taken them from the safety of the bigger boat, one with a radio and a GPS, a tad prematurely.

But he'd heard the captain order the evacuation, even with his hearing aids turned down. He had. He'd seen the flashing lights, witnessed the lights on the boat go out, heard the cry of everyone still on board.

Foolishness hit him, further silencing him. Eventually, Iris turned and walked up the beach, leaving Justin to follow in her wake this time.

Hours later, as the sun sank into the ocean on his right, Justin finished tying the last string of bark around the branches he'd pulled down to make a shelter. He didn't want to sleep in sand, and the raised platform would keep them dry as well.

His fingers had been bleeding as he ripped tree bark into strings, as he pulled branches from trees strong enough to hold their combined body weight. Everything hurt, and Iris stepped over to him and put her hand on his shoulder.

"Take these." She held out a palm full of pills and an expandable plastic cup of water.

"You filtered that?"

"There was a single bottle of water in my hip pack," she said. "But I'm going to figure out how to filter in the morning." She offered him a weak smile, and Justin found it lovely in the waning sunlight.

He accepted the pills, swallowed them, and collapsed onto the shelter. He'd positioned two tree limbs at almost ninety-degree angles and draped the biggest palm fronds he could find from one branch to another to create a roof.

The platform was barely big enough for him, but Iris was slight and petite, and she'd fit against him just fine.

He breathed in and out, in and out, hoping the

medicine would spread through him quickly. "We'll search for fruit trees in the morning," he said. "And I'm sure we can figure out the filtration system."

Iris sat on the edge of the platform with her back to him, the breeze playing with her hair. "I can't believe this is my vacation."

"First time on a cruise," he said, chuckling.

She turned and glared at him, but it only lasted a moment before her face dissolved into a smile too. And with that, she tucked herself into his chest, and Justin closed his eyes, hoping sleep would claim him tonight when it hadn't last night.

CHAPTER FIVE

*I*ris woke long before the sun, but Justin's even breathing and steady rise and fall of his chest indicated that he was still asleep. She enjoyed the weight of his arm over her waist, the heat of him behind her.

A smile touched her lips. Maybe this wasn't how she wanted to spend her vacation. She wondered if Sam and Betty had even thought about her. She wondered where everyone else had gone in their lifeboats, and if they'd managed to stay together.

She needed to use the bathroom and figure out how to make the sea water drinkable. Eden had taught her enough to know that water was more important than food. She slipped from under Justin's arm and went out into the forested part of the island, looking back every so often to make sure she didn't get lost.

She relieved herself and went back for her hip pack,

intending to fill that collapsible cup many times over before the end of the day. Humming to herself, she didn't realize Justin was up until she reached the platform and found it empty.

Anxiety sprang through her, and she glanced around. "Justin?" Maybe he'd had to use the bathroom too. Her hip pack wasn't hanging on the pole where she'd put it, and she bent to look in the sand.

"I have it," Justin said, and she glanced up to see him walking toward her, shirt off.

Iris could only stare, dry-mouthed, as he approached. He held out her hip pack. "You're looking for this, right?"

She only took the pack because he would've dropped it if she hadn't. "Yeah," she managed to say stupidly.

"So we have shelter," he said. "Up next is water."

"I can do it," she said, wondering why he needed her pack that morning. "I didn't wake you when I got up, did I?"

"No," he said simply. "I think it wise to stay out of the sun as much as possible today."

Iris didn't like how he said things like they were law, and she took her pack toward the water's edge. "I'll get us something to drink." She marched away from him, the rising sun already heating the sand.

So maybe he was right. Maybe it would be in their best interest to have a quick drink and lay around in the shade for most of the day.

"And do what?" she muttered. "Talk?" More like he'd boss her around, expecting her to do everything he said, when he said it.

She pulled out the water filtration system and unfolded the instructions. Half of them were in Spanish, and she turned them over to find the English section. This was a solar-powered desalination kit, and it said it could take several hours to get drinking water.

Her hopes fell, but she filled the bag the way the directions said to and set it in the sun, also according to the instructions. Her mouth felt like she'd brushed her teeth with sand, and she mourned the thought that she wouldn't be able to properly care for her teeth in the immediate future.

Justin approached, and Iris didn't want to tell him there would be no drink water until afternoon. If then. So she said nothing.

"Solar-powered?" he asked.

"Yes." She brought her knees to her chest and stared out at the water. "Justin, where is everyone else?"

"I don't know." He sat down beside her and gazed at the ocean too. "I can go see what I can find us to eat." He stood up again. "Don't stay out here too long. I really do worry about you in the sun."

With that, he walked away, the sand making shifting sounds as he did. Iris stayed for another moment, and then she scrambled to her feet. She didn't want to be left alone, and she caught up to him by jogging several steps.

"So," she said, blowing out her breath and wishing a little running in the sand didn't leave her so winded. "Do you have a girlfriend back in Getaway Bay?"

Justin looked down at her out of the corner of his eyes. "Going right for the jugular, aren't we?"

Iris didn't know what that meant. "I'm sorry?" He seemed to be walking so fast now. So fast, and Iris couldn't keep up.

Relief met her under the shade of the trees, and still Justin hadn't answered her. She wasn't sure why she was surprised. Maybe because she'd thought they were getting along. He may have gotten them to this island, but she had all the supplies in the hip pack. She'd worked just as hard as he had on the shelter yesterday, dragging branches through sand as if both surfaces were well-lubricated.

She'd ripped tree bark too. She'd held pieces in place while he tied everything together. She wasn't as strong as he was, but it had taken both of them to build that shelter.

"Coconuts," he said, pointing up. "How good are you at climbing trees?"

"You're joking, right?"

Of course he was, because he stretched his arms and started for the tree. He scaled it as if he were part monkey and started throwing down coconuts. She got out of the way, grabbing one that rolled in her direction. She could open this. She would. She'd show Justin that she could do important tasks, just like him.

But she'd forgotten the all-in-one tool back at camp. It was fine. She could use the collapsible cup. She could.

In the end, he was the one who stabbed the end of the collapsible cup into the top of the coconut and then broke it open on the ground. He held the two pieces in two different hands and handed her one. "Drink the water."

"I don't like coconut water."

He gave her a nasty look. "Drink it or die."

She wasn't sure where the kind, compassionate man had gone, but she much preferred him to this bossy, meatheaded Navy SEAL.

"What does SEAL stand for in Navy SEAL anyway?" she asked, lifting the coconut to her lips. The coconut water tasted bitter in her mouth, but she supposed he was right. She needed to eat and drink, and this was what they had.

"Sea, air, and land," he said. "We're trained to navigate obstacles and run missions in all conditions." Their eyes met, and Iris could appreciate his good looks. But no amount of handsome made up for a salty personality.

"Have you ever navigated a deserted island?" she asked.

"I can't say that I have." He chipped away at the coconut in his part of the shell with a pair of nail clippers he'd found in her hip pack. He'd at least given her the spoon, so maybe chivalry wasn't dead.

"I didn't mean anything by asking you about your girlfriend," she said, trying to get the tension between them to dissipate. "I'm sure she's great."

"I don't have a girlfriend," he said.

"Then why'd you get all bent out of shape when I asked?"

"Did I?"

"You said I went right for the jugular. Did you… have a bad experience or something?"

Justin continued to eat, a flush creeping up his neck and into his cheeks. Or maybe he was just sunburned. Iris wasn't sure.

"I don't have a girlfriend," he said. "And not much experience with women at all." Their eyes met, and he quickly looked back at his coconut.

"Really?" she asked, surprise streaming through her. "Why not?"

"I served in the military for two decades," he said. "I didn't think I had time for a girl." He shrugged. "I didn't want to drag a family all over the place, and I didn't want someone at home, worrying about me."

Iris kept her attention down too, trying to figure out how she felt about what he'd said. "It's nice to have someone at home, worrying about you." She thought of her parents, of how worried they'd all been when Eden was stuck up on the bluffs. At least then, she'd called and texted. They knew where she was and that she was alive.

Her emotions choked in her throat, making eating the coconut impossible. Her family had no idea where she was right now, or if she was even alive. "I can't imagine how my family is taking this news." She sniffled, because she'd let her emotions out in her voice already.

Justin reached over and squeezed her hand. "We'll survive this, Iris. We have food. We have water. Or we will have. And we have shelter."

"I'm scared," she admitted, still unable to look at him.

"I've been in dozens of situations that scared me," he said gently. "We can beat this."

She looked at him then, finding the sheer determination in his gaze. He was strong and capable, and she nodded. "I'm trying."

Confusion rippled his eyebrows. "Did I say you weren't?"

"No," she said. "I just...can't do everything you can do."

"You're doing fine," he said, chipping away at his coconut again. "So, just your family will be worried about you? No boyfriend in the picture?"

She could've imagined the interest in his voice, but Iris had some experience with men and flirting.

"Oh, I'm married to my business," she said, almost hoping that would get him to back off. Or did she want him to pursue her? "I own We'll Weed That, and it's a busy job."

He glanced at her again. "So no boyfriend."

"No," she said.

"Have you tried that dating app?"

"No," she said again. "But my twin sister has."

"Twin sister. Wow." He smiled. "Does she look like you?"

"We're mirror twins," she said. "So very close, but her hair parts on the left, mine on the right. Stuff like that." And Ivy had been messaging several men through Getaway Bay Singles, and she'd liked it. Told Iris all about it.

"Ivy loves the app," she said. "She's gone on a few dates, but I don't think she's found anyone she quite likes very much." She liked this easier conversation. "She did mention a guy she's been talking with a lot, but he hasn't asked her out yet. Is that normal? How much do you talk to someone before you ask them out?"

He cleared his throat. "I haven't actually asked anyone out yet."

His nerves about women were actually kind of cute. "No? Why not?"

"I'm just testing things out for now," he said. "I've only been using the app for a few weeks."

"Yeah? But you like it?"

"I mean, my boss developed it. I work for The Web Developer now. That's why I was on the cruise."

"That's right." Iris finished with her coconut, her stomach starting to rebel at all the sweet starch. She leaned against the tree trunk behind her and watched Justin. A body as big and buff as his would need more than coconuts. "Tell me who you've been talking to on the app."

"Oh, I don't know," he said. "A couple of people. I'm honestly not on my phone that much."

"Ivy's been messaging a guy called Frogman." Iris giggled, the name still funny to her. "I think it's kind of weird that anyone can assume any name. She doesn't even know who he is."

Justin slowly lifted his eyes to hers. "Frogman?"

"Yeah," Iris said, noting the sparks in his eyes. She leaned toward him, trying to decipher his expression.

"Is your sister PoisonedApple?"

Iris didn't know what to say.

Justin started to chuckle, shaking his head as he went back to his coconut shell. "What are the odds of that?"

"You know her?" Iris's voice was barely more than a whisper. This really was a nightmare. A living nightmare. Her twin sister had been chatting it up with Justin, and now she was stranded with him on a deserted island.

And crushing on him. Hard.

"We've been chatting," he said. "I haven't asked her out."

"Do you want to ask her out?" Iris didn't mean to practically yell the words.

Justin looked at her, a perfect storm moving across his face. "Honestly? Yeah, eventually, I would've probably asked her out."

Iris felt like crying, and she didn't even know why. She'd spent a couple of nights with this guy, and she barely knew him. So he was attractive. He had a bark and probably a bite, and all she had to do was survive this island and get back to her real life.

She stood up, her stomach sloshing now for an entirely new reason. "Excuse me."

"Iris," he called after her, but she just kept walking. Back at the shelter, she grabbed her phone from the hip pack and walked along the edge of the trees. Her phone had no service, but it had a charge, and she typed out a journal entry in her note app, hoping it would bleed away the negativity brewing within her.

Leave it to me to have feelings for a man my sister is already messaging…

ustin wanted to go after Iris, but he also wanted more than coconut to eat. He sighed, because the woman could move fast when she wanted to.

The truth was, he'd started to think maybe he and Iris could have something. Yes, he'd been messaging her sister—but he hadn't known that. He hadn't asked her out.

"But she wanted you to," he muttered as he piled as many coconuts into his arms as he could carry. He took them back to the shelter and lined them up on the platform. "And you should've lied," he scolded himself. "Told her, 'of course I don't want to ask out your *twin sister*.' Jeez." He scanned for Iris afterward. He couldn't see her, which was good. Sort of.

At least it meant she'd stayed in the shade, out of

the sun. The water filtration system still sat in the sun, and he checked it to find a couple of cups of water already accumulated. Also good.

He'd find more food and find something to put the drinkable water in, and then he'd make more. That would be a task they'd have to constantly be on top of, but hey, it gave him something to do.

In Justin's opinion, there was nothing worse than being idle. Having nothing to do. "Iris?" he called, and he heard her say, "Over here," to his right.

He went that way, scanning the forest for her. After only a minute, he found her sitting in the sand, her back against a tree, tapping on her phone.

"Hey," he said softly, the way he would to a scared animal he wanted to coax over to him. "Can I talk to you for a sec?"

"Sure," she said brightly, as if she hadn't just told him he'd been flirting with her sister through a dating app.

"I'm going to go look for more fruit," he said. "I could use the help."

"All right." She got up, stuffed her phone in her back pocket, and brushed off her shorts. "Let's go."

He stepped, and she did too, and Justin deliberately reached over and took her hand in his. Iris stilled, and then tried to pull her hand away.

"I'm not going to ask your sister out," he said, fixing his eyes on her and begging silently that she'd look at him.

Whether it was the weight of his stare or her own curiosity, it didn't matter. She looked at him. "Yeah? Why not?"

"Because I'm sort of interested in someone else."

"Another woman on your app?" Her eyes threw flames at him, and Justin found he wanted to get burned by her.

"A woman I met on a cruise," he said, a smile spreading across his face. "She asks sort of blunt questions, but she's pretty, and I like talking to her."

Iris blinked, pure shock flowing across her fair features now. He reached over with his free hand and tucked her hair behind her ear. "I'm talking about you, by the way."

"You think I'm pretty?"

"See what I mean about the blunt questions?" He shook his head, tugged on her hand to get her walking again, and said, "Yes, Iris. I think you're pretty." The blonde hair, the freckles splashed across her cheeks, the curve in her hips. What wasn't to like?

She squeezed his hand, and he took that as her saying, *I think you're handsome*, or something. He wasn't sure if Iris would actually call him handsome. Good-looking? Hot? Either way, she was interested in him too.

They walked through the trees, finding more coconuts. "There has to be mango or banana or something on this island," he said. He'd tried a plethora of fruits since living in Getaway Bay, and there had to be more here than coconuts.

Up the swell they went, and back down the other side. "Over there," Iris said, and she let go of his hand to veer right.

"What is it?" he asked as she started jogging toward a squatty tree that looked like it had flat cactus growing from it.

"Dragon fruit," she said, turning back to him with triumph on her face. She picked the spiky, pink fruit and handed it to him. "They're really good."

"I've had dragon fruit," he said. "Once or twice. I don't eat the skin, right?"

"No," she said. "You cut it open. Like a kiwi."

He didn't have a knife, so he dug his fingernails into the skin of the fruit and broke it open. The flesh was white, with black seeds throughout. He didn't care what it looked like. It smelled like pears and honeydew, and he took a big bite. A groan of pleasure leaked through his lips. "This is great."

She nodded, eating her way through her own dragon fruit. Once they finished, she pulled out the purple top of her pj's. "Let's load up as many as we can in this."

"Genius." He got to work picking as much of the fruit as they could carry. "We can come back for more later."

"I think I see something else down there," she said,

peering further into the forest. "Should we check it out?"

"We have nothing else to do," he said.

She laid their dragon fruit haul on the ground and led him past a few more trees to another type of tree. Almost a bust, really.

"I think this is rambutan," she said. "My father had a tree like this in our backyard for a while. He hated it. Said it dropped too much fruit."

"Too much fruit sounds amazing," Justin said, reaching out to pick one of the small spheres. They were grouped in huge bunches, with tons of spiny things coming off of them. No bigger than an egg, the fruit fit in the palm of his hand, and he tried to break it open the way he had the dragon fruit. But the skin came away easily, and he almost smashed the fruit inside.

"I've never had this," he said, looking at Iris.

She squeezed her rambutan, and the flesh came popping right out of the pink skin. "It's good," she said, taking a bite of the pale flesh. Another bite, and the fruit was gone. "Try it."

He did, getting the flavor of a red grape. "Mm." He finished his. "Not as juicy as a grape. But good." They were small enough, he could probably eat the whole tree by himself.

"Let's take the dragon fruit back and come back for these," she said. "It'll give us a little variety, at least."

He agreed, and they'd taken two steps when a crack sounded in the forest beyond them. They both froze as if in unison. "What was that?" Iris asked.

"I don't know," Justin whispered, searching the forest around him. It sounded like someone crashing through undergrowth, but there wasn't much of that here. He took another step, hoping there weren't rats or rabbits on this island. The creatures dominated the populated islands, as did birds, mongoose, and feral populations of donkeys, goats, and pigs.

He'd take a pig, but he thought it unlikely he'd find one out here. There had to be people to bring the pigs to the island in the first place, and he wasn't sure a human had been on this island before.

"Come on," he said, nodding to Iris like she was one of his SEAL teammates and she'd understand his nonverbal cues to move. She seemed to do just fine, and they made it back to the dragon fruit tree and the stash they'd been planning to take back.

He didn't see anything. No prints. No evidence that anyone or anything had been there, except for them.

He scooped up the purple silk full of fruit and turned to her just as she said, "Justin."

He didn't need her to say anything else. "It's a nene," he said, staring at the native Hawaiian goose. They were rare, and he'd only seen one in the zoo. "Wow."

"Maybe this island is part of its nesting grounds," she whispered.

"Maybe," he said. He didn't think they needed to fear a goose, but he kept his eyes on it as they started back toward their shelter. The bird just stood there and watched them, and finally, Justin tuned his back on it and increased his pace.

Iris gave a shaky laugh. "I don't know what I thought it was," she said. "But I was thinking you know, Godzilla or something."

Justin laughed with her, though he was also glad the noise had just been a goose. "Gotta be alert at all times, I guess."

They dropped off their fruit and went back for the rambutan. The nene wasn't to be found, and Iris made him go all the way to the other side of the island. "This place is tiny," she said. "I bet we could walk the circumference of the whole thing in a couple of hours."

"Probably," he agreed.

When she met his eye, she wore worry on her face. "If it's so small, how will anyone find us?"

He didn't know, but he didn't want to tell her that. So he said, "They'll find us, Iris," and hurried back to the shelter. He wasn't sure why, but he wanted to be on this side of the island, where he could see the water where they'd come in.

Help would come from that direction, he was sure of it.

THE NEXT MORNING, HE AND IRIS NOSHED ON dragon fruit and rambutan. They set more ocean water to evaporate into drinking water in the filtration system, and he did take her hand and say, "Let's see how long it takes us to walk the island."

Less than two hours. They stayed under the trees, almost out in the sun. She found sea grapes in one spot, and he scaled the only banana tree they could find to get as much fruit from it as they could.

He kept his eyes peeled for anything they could use to boil water, but there was nothing. No pots. No shells. Nothing watertight that could withstand fire. Not that they had fire. But he could make it if he had to.

The sun kept them plenty warm during the day, and they kept each other warm at night. Justin was used to sleeping in horrible conditions, without a blanket for comfort. But Iris confessed she wasn't, and he let her gripe about how the sand scratched her and how tight her sunburned skin was.

"Let's make hats this afternoon," he said. "And we'll eat a couple of protein cookies, and things will be okay."

She nodded, turned away from him, and sniffed. He let her have a moment to weep, because he knew how overwhelming a situation could be. They'd been on the island for just over twenty-four hours and away from the cruise ship for two whole days.

While she went to take care of her bathroom needs, he stood at the shelter and gazed at the ocean in front of him. It was huge. He was not. The island was not.

"How are they ever going to find us?" he whispered. "Please, Lord, help them find us."

CHAPTER SEVEN

Iris wasn't a religious person, but when she heard Justin's plea to the Lord to help their rescuers find them, she added her own prayer to his.

He put on a really good front, she'd give him that. He was all assurances and reassurances. *We have food. We have water. We'll be okay.*

And she'd believed him. It was easier than believing she was going to die on this island.

And at least she wasn't alone.

"Okay," she said, returning to the shelter and causing him to turn toward her. "I don't know how to make a hat." She looked at him expectantly, and he sat on the edge of the platform they'd built.

"I don't either," he said. "But we can start by weaving some fronds together. Something that will keep the sun off our faces and shoulders while we're out working."

She wasn't sure what work they had to do. The island was providing enough food and water for them, and they didn't have tools to build with. Could she really live her whole life on this platform? She couldn't wear the same clothes forever. Could she?

She put the thoughts out of her mind. "Tell me about your family," she said, needing a conversation to drive away the worry.

"I'm the oldest," he said.

"Big shocker," she teased, and he smiled.

"Two younger sisters. Star and Kaylee. My mother passed away a couple of years ago. Dad is dating someone new. They all live in North Carolina."

"Everyone but you?"

"Yeah," he said. "I grew up near Fort Bragg there. Loved swimming and water polo in high school, and joined the Navy the first chance I got." He grinned as if his time in the Navy had been the highlight of his life. Maybe it had been.

"That's great," she said.

"What about you?"

She told him about her two older sisters. Skimmed over Ivy, only saying she was older by four minutes, and said, "We grew up in Getaway Bay, and we all live there still."

"You're close to your family."

"Yes," she said, the word sticking in her throat. "Very."

"My unit was like family to me," he said, his voice

somewhat cooler than it had been a moment ago. "I miss being part of something like that." Justin rarely let her see a vulnerable side of him, and she paused in her useless weaving to look at him. He kept his eyes on his work, but she sensed a gentle soul inside the tough Navy man.

"You don't see them anymore?"

"I retired," he said. "I still see some of them, sure. But it's not the same." He flashed her a smile and went back to the leaves in front of him. "You like owning your own company?"

"It's a lot of work," she admitted, maybe for the first time.

"Sounds like you don't like it."

"I do," she said, wishing her voice didn't stray up an octave. "It's just a lot of work. It's kind of like how you said you didn't have time for a girl in the Navy. That's how I feel with We'll Weed That."

He nodded, and she noticed the way he pressed his lips together, almost like he had something to say and was physically trying not to say it.

"What?" she asked.

"Nothing."

"Justin." She put her hand on his to get him to stop. "What?"

Their eyes met, and he looked angry. Actually angry. She pulled her hand back as if his skin had burned her.

"I guess I'm just wondering what we're doing," he said.

Confusion knotted her stomach. "What do you mean?"

"I mean, I told you I was interested in you, and now you're telling me you don't have time for anything but your business."

"I told you I was married to it," she said.

"I thought that was, you know, figurative."

Iris didn't know what to say. Did she have to work as much as she did? Probably not.

Definitely not, her mind whispered. But she didn't exactly have a whole lot to go home to, and maybe it was easier to stay at work sometimes.

"Never mind," he said, his voice on the harsh side now. "Thank you for telling me before things went too far."

"Justin," she said, but she didn't know what else to add. Finally, she asked, "What would've been too far?"

"I don't know. Kissing you."

"Oh, so that's not going to happen." She didn't phrase it as a question, and she threw a smile in his direction, not really checking to make sure he'd received it.

"I don't—you *want* that to happen?"

"I'm not working right now," she said. "I mean, besides this pathetic attempt at weaving a hat." She held up her art project, but the weave wasn't tight enough and it almost fell apart.

"But what about when we get back?" he asked.

"Do you always think ten steps ahead?" she asked.

"No."

But she thought he did. He'd probably had to as a SEAL. "Tell me about one of your missions."

That got him talking about something else. While he obviously left out a lot of details, at least he wasn't brooding anymore.

Iris did, though, because yes. She wanted that kiss from him. The thought of going back to Getaway Bay and having him message Ivy made every cell in her turn sour.

She wove until he finished talking, and she was nowhere near making a hat. "I think I'll use this as a bedroll," she said. "And you know what? We should go cut some of those dragon fruit leaves. They were thick and would probably make this platform less like sleeping on logs." Because it was like sleeping on logs.

"Good idea," he said. "You've got the knife this time?"

"Yes," she said, reaching into her hip pack and pulling it out. Eden really had prepared her well for the trip—but only if she took the tools with her.

A couple of hours later, their shelter had been drastically improved by the addition of the palm frond mats and the dragon fruit leaves. They were long pieces of near-rubber, somewhat like a flattened cactus without the spines.

"So much better," she said with a smile as she stretched out on the padded logs. "I'm going to sleep great tonight."

She hoped. She hadn't the past couple of nights, though she did doze at least a little.

"We should probably have a little to drink," Justin said, and Iris slipped off the platform to follow him.

He poured her a cup of water and watched her drink it before he did the same. "It's not great warm, is it?"

"Nope." Iris didn't want to complain, but ice would be a drastic improvement to this island experience. As would air conditioning. She thought of all the modern conveniences she normally took for granted, and she vowed that when she got back to Getaway Bay, she wouldn't be like that anymore.

Justin filled the filtration system with more ocean water, and they retreated back to the shade. "I'm going to take a nap," he said with a yawn.

"Can I join you?" she asked.

"Sure." He stretched out on the platform, a sigh leaking from his mouth.

Iris lay down beside him, barely enough room for her there. She adjusted her body, and her hand touched his. He started to pull away, but Iris kept her fingers firmly in his.

He turned toward her, and she said, "I do want that kiss at some point, Frogman." She wasn't normally so bold and forward, but it seemed like Justin needed something straightforward to latch onto.

"Maybe just put it in your plan," she said. "For the future."

"How far in the future?" he asked.

"I don't know." She closed her eyes and smiled. "You're the planner, not me."

He chuckled, lifted her fingers to his lips, and settled down to sleep. Iris did too, but fantasies of him kissing her while their legs tangled in the hot island sand kept her awake long after his breathing had evened.

WHEN IRIS WOKE, SHE WAS ALONE IN THE shelter. The wind had picked up, and her hip pack flapped against the pole. The noise had disturbed her sleep, and now she looked around, almost desperate to find Justin.

Because if there was anything worse than being stuck on a deserted island, it was having to be alone. She'd seen the movies. People went crazy out here by themselves.

She stood up and rubbed her hands up and down her arms, though it wasn't exactly cold. In that moment, she realized clouds had gathered in the sky. It was going to rain.

And rain meant drinking water.

Her pulse pounded in her temples. They needed to gather as much rainwater as they could. Then they could drink more than a couple of cups each day. Frantically, she looked around their camp, as if a bucket or a barrel had magically appeared during her nap.

Of course, nothing had.

Desperation clogged her throat as her eyes landed on the mats she and Justin had woven. They'd hold water. Wouldn't they?

She shoved off the dragon fruit leaf pad and snatched up the two mats she and Justin had made. She could make boats out of them. Hammocks. Something that would hold the water when it fell.

Working quickly, she tied one end of her mat to the outside pole of the shelter. It wasn't big enough to reach the next tree truck, but she had the nylon cord from her survival kit. With that, she managed to get the mat strung up between the two items.

She didn't care if she had to stand in the rain and coax the mat into the right shape to hold the water. In fact, she'd do it with an open mouth.

A gust of wind picked up, almost blowing Iris away as she reached up to steady the mat. The first raindrops fell, and she made sure the mat was open at the top, exactly like a hammock.

The water felt good on her scorched skin, and she turned her face into the rain as it fell. A smile touched her lips, and she turned when she heard Justin yell her name.

"Here," she called, waving as he came out of the jungle. "It's raining."

He dropped the load of rambutan and dragon fruit he'd been off collecting and ran for the filtration system they left out in the sun.

He poured the filtered water into a coconut half-shell they'd been using as a cup and set out several others they'd cleaned out too. "Great idea with the mat," he said, glancing at their shelter. It wasn't water-proof at all, but right now, Iris didn't care.

Justin opened the bag he usually filled with sea water and held it open for the rainwater to fall into as well.

Iris met his eye, and the two of them started laughing. If anyone could see them, they'd be laughing too. It was quite comical to have them both standing out in the rain, holding open any container they could find and getting soaking wet.

CHAPTER EIGHT

The storm passed quickly, but Justin estimated they'd collected several cups of water from the microburst. His stomach cringed at the idea of eating dragon fruit for dinner, but he had no other choice. Well, a rambutan.

As the rain stopped, Iris slowly lowered her hand, testing to see if the mat would hold the water without her help. It did, and she sighed as she wiped both hands through her hair. She was shapely with her clothes stuck to her, and sexy with that water dripping from her face.

Justin looked away, his fantasies once again flying into overdrive. But she'd said—twice—that she was married to her company. He'd watched Theo and his wife go through some hard things with regard to how much his boss worked, and Justin didn't want that kind of relationship.

He didn't need a woman waiting at home for him either, but the idea wasn't all bad in his mind. Iris had pegged him correctly when she'd said he planned ten steps ahead. When she'd said she wanted him to kiss her, he'd paused to try to figure out how to make that step one.

Napping had won out over simply lunging at her, and Justin was still trying to figure out when a kiss between them would be appropriate.

"That was awesome," she said, twirling in the sand, laughter bubbling from her throat. Justin moved over to the coconut shells and combined them as much as possible so he could pour the rainwater from the filtration bag into the empty ones.

No sense in thinking they had all the water they needed. With another night approaching, and then another morning, another day, Justin had to start thinking long-term.

Unable to sleep, he'd walked the island again, and there was nothing in any direction. Not another smidge of land on the horizon. No evidence of other human life previous to them. Nothing but ocean in all directions.

The fruit trees puzzled him, but he supposed the wind could carry seeds a long way. He was grateful they had what they did, but he felt weaker with every passing day that he didn't eat protein.

With the water situation handled, he turned to Iris. She sat on the edge of the platform, looking out at the ocean. "The waves seem angry," she said.

He followed her gaze. "They do." He drew in a deep breath and sat next to her. "For dinner tonight, we have the option of dragon fruit," he said in a game show host voice. "Or rambutan. Which will you pick?"

She looked at him and laughed, and Justin decided their situation could definitely be worse. Neither of them were injured too badly—just a sunburn from the first day on the boat that was already starting to fade. There was no snow. And no one trying to kill them.

"Rambutan for me," she said. "To start. After that, I think I'll have the...dragon fruit." She gave him a sly smile, and Justin returned it before handing her a bunch of rambutan.

"I've been thinking," he said as he used the all-in-one tool to slice open dragon fruit appetizer. "At some point, we're going to have to consider leaving this island."

She jerked her eyes to his. "What?"

He nodded toward the boat. "We have the boat. I can get us back over the break." At least he hoped he could. Not in weather like this, with a wind blowing from the west that could chap a man's face.

"And we head south again. We came north to find this place. So we go south, and we should run back into Maui."

"We should?" She shook her head. "I don't like the sound of that. You have no idea where we are."

No, he didn't. "But the archipelago of islands is south," he said. "We'll have to hit it eventually."

"So…what? We just load up onto the boat and sail for days in the sun?" She looked at his face and then his arms. "You're still burnt from last time."

"I just don't know how much longer we can stay here," he said. "That's all. I'm just thinking ahead." He popped a bite of fruit into his mouth. They could load up all the water they could carry with them. All the dragon fruit the boat would hold. And just go. At least then, he'd feel like he was doing something besides waiting for someone to come find them.

They ate in silence, and Justin hated that he'd caused it. But someone had to start thinking long-term, and it wasn't going to be Iris.

"How long do you think we should wait?" she finally asked. "Like, let's agree on a day."

Justin shrugged one shoulder, as if he'd never thought of it. "It's what? Day three here?"

"It's night three," she said. "Day three will be tomorrow."

"Okay," he said. "Assuming that cruise line discovered we were gone on the first day, there should be a boat already out looking. We got here in a tiny lifeboat in about twelve hours. A big, powerful boat with an engine? Shouldn't take nearly as long."

He hoped she understood what he was really saying. The ocean was huge. Their island was small. It could be very possible that they'd never be found.

"Maybe we should build a fire," she suggested.

"Send up some kind of signal someone could see from far away."

"That's a good idea," he said. "I can do that in the morning." He finished his last piece of fruit, nowhere near satisfied but unable to put another bite in his mouth. "I think we plan to evacuate on day seven. Think about it, Iris. We can't be that far from a populated island."

She kept her head down but looked up at him. "How far?"

"If I keep the boat moving south, I think we'd only need to be on it for a day. Tops. Twelve hours to get here, heading due north. We couldn't have been that far from Maui when those whales attacked. The course took us right along the north side of it."

He shouldn't have taken them north. He knew it, and he wondered if Iris did too. Surely she did. She wasn't stupid.

She nodded, her mouth a tight line. "Okay," she said. "Day seven."

"Okay," he echoed, looking down to the boat on the beach. Day seven gave him enough time to fashion a canopy for the boat. Something they could hunker down under to stay out of the sun. He'd weave whatever leaves and branches together that he had to, and he'd find a way to keep the drinking water pure as well.

He had to.

Because he didn't think help was coming.

THE NEXT MORNING, HE SAWED AT THE branches of a nearby banyan tree, choosing skinnier ones he could add to the boat without putting too much weight on it. Without a hammer and nails, everything had to be lashed together, but the palm tree bark ripped easily enough and stayed in long strips.

Iris collected their drinking water and set out more to filter. She went into the forest alone and returned with more fruit. She came down to the boat and held things in place while he tied and tightened.

He told her about his friends still in the SEALs, only mentioning the good things or the funny situations they'd found themselves in. Number one, most of what he'd done for a living was classified, and number two, he missed his old life in the Navy.

Talking about it with her helped, and she seemed to enjoy his stories.

"Will I get to meet this Heath Hawkins?" she asked. "He seems like a real character."

"Heath's great," Justin said. "And yeah, I imagine you'll meet him." He pulled the last binding tight and stood back. "There. We have four poles over the boat now."

His fingers ached, but Iris hopped out of the boat like they hadn't been working all morning. She bumped him with her hip. "Is the meeting going to happen before or after you kiss me?"

"Oh, you're still hung up on that."

"I'm just saying it's private out here," she said as she started up the beach toward the shelter.

That it was. Justin chuckled as he followed her, catching up to her easily. He took her hand in his and tugged her close to his side. "Maybe you should stop badgering me about kissing you."

"Badgering you?"

"Maybe I have something romantic planned," he said. "And you're just making it harder to do."

"Romantic?" she brushed her hair out of her eyes as they arrived at camp. "I know it can't be roses and chocolates. Or even dinner." She gave him a playful smile, and Justin decided to abandon all his plans.

He put his free hand on the tree trunk beside her head and leaned down. She froze, her eyes searching his. "You're absolutely maddening," he whispered, ducking his head closer to her, noticing that she closed her eyes and waited.

He drew out the moment, really making her wait for him, and then he brushed his lips across hers. Sparks of light popped behind his closed eyes, and a growl tore through his throat. He cupped her face and kissed her, thrilled when she moved her hands through his hair, down the back of his neck.

Pressing her into the tree behind her, he kissed her deeper, wondering why he'd waited so long to abandon his plans and make her his.

And the best part?

She kissed him back with an equal amount of passion, power, and pure desire in her touch.

CHAPTER NINE

*I*ris had never been kissed the way Justin kissed her. She held onto his shoulders, trying to enjoy the ride before she had to get off. He was utterly in control, though she fought him for it every step of the way.

If he didn't have her pressed against the tree, she wouldn't be able to stand, and when he finally pulled away, she still wanted more.

He kept his face very close to hers, and she didn't dare open her eyes yet. "Passable?" he whispered, his lips catching on her earlobe and making her shiver.

"Mm," was all she could come up with. His touch felt like silk on her waist, and she didn't dare move so he'd keep doing whatever he was doing to her. Stars seemed to beam through her whole body, and she wanted to feel this adored every day of her life.

"I haven't kissed anyone for a while," he said, finally putting a few inches between them.

"Well, you're not rusty at all." She opened her eyes to see him run one hand up the back of his neck, as if nervous.

"No?"

Iris grinned at him. "Were you nervous?"

"Yes." He smiled back at her, his dark eyes devouring her. "You're surprised by that?"

"Yeah," she said, trying to lift one shoulder into a shrug as casually as he did. "You're this big, buff, tattooed Navy SEAL. I'm just…Iris."

He touched his lips to her forehead, and then her cheekbone. "You're smart, and sexy, and you scare me."

She put her hands back on those broad, decorated shoulders. "How do I scare you?"

"You just do," he said, backing up fully now. He kept his eyes low too, and Iris sensed he had a secret he wasn't willing to share yet.

Which was fine, honestly.

They had four more days on this island, and she'd get it out of him soon enough.

IN THE MIDDLE OF THE NIGHT, IRIS LAY IN THE safety of Justin's arms, his breath falling softly against her shoulder as she gazed up into the starry sky. She felt utterly alone, though she wasn't. It was a strange feeling that moved through her powerfully and made her shiver.

Instantly, Justin pulled her closer, his lips touching her shoulder. "You okay?" he whispered.

At least now she knew he wasn't asleep—and that he was very good at pretending he was. "Do you ever wonder what you're doing here?" she asked him. "I mean, even the sky is this huge thing. And we're just…nothing."

"Mm," he said, his voice definitely sleepy. "It's easy to feel insignificant."

"Yes, insignificant." That was how she felt. She liked to think her company would fall apart without her, but deep down, she knew they wouldn't. "Like, what have I done with my life?"

"Plenty," he said. "You own your own company, Iris. That's huge."

"You served your country for two decades. That's something, at least."

Justin didn't move behind her. "How old are you?"

"Thirty-one," she said.

"You've still got time to do something amazing," he said. "If that's what you want. I think you're doing just fine."

She sighed and snuggled into him, the stars still staring her in the face. "Do you think there's more out there?"

"Like, God?" he asked.

"Yeah," she said.

"I don't know," he said. "I knew lots of guys who believed in God. They said it was easier than not, especially seeing some of the stuff we see."

"I don't think anyone's going to find us," she whispered, true worrying running through her now.

Several long seconds passed before Justin said, "I don't think so either."

She twisted in his arms. "We should go as soon as the boat is ready."

He looked down at her, and now the starlight glinted in his eyes. He was gorgeous, and she believed him when he said he could get them back to a populated island. "You think so?"

"We could work all day tomorrow and set out at night," she said. "Less time in the sun."

"Yeah," he said, but doubt resided in his voice. "I'm worried I won't be able to navigate as well at night."

"Sea, air, and land, right?" she asked. "You didn't learn how to navigate by the stars."

"I did, yes," he said. "SEAL training is two and a half years."

"Wow," she said. "That's crazy."

"It was intense," he agreed. "Let's see how tomorrow plays out. We need to make sure we have enough food and water, as well as adequate shelter."

"Okay." She cuddled into his chest, his arm a much softer pillow than the logs. He pressed a kiss to her temple, and finally, she slept.

THE NEXT DAY FELT LIKE WATER SLIPPING through her fingers. She felt an inexplicable need to get off the island, so she worked at a feverish pace. Weaving fronds together for the whole morning left her with a canopy big enough to stretch from pole to pole, but then she and Justin couldn't get it to stay up. The boat was too long, and it needed a pole in the middle.

Justin worked on that, but there was nothing to lash it to. Not really. The bench where he needed to sit to row didn't provide any height. They pulled it tight, thinking maybe if they just got it taut enough, the four corners would keep it up.

As a few of the fronds ripped, he said, "Stop. Stop, stop, stop," in his barking, military voice.

Frustration roared through Iris. At him. At the stupid palm fronds. At this idiotic island.

"I'll fix it," she said, dragging the canopy up the beach to the shade. Justin had been weaving bark into holders for the coconut shells. She didn't see how they'd make it over the break with any water in them at all, but she didn't say anything.

Justin wasn't stupid. He knew what it took to get over the break, and that they'd have only the filtration kit to make more water.

She worked in the shade while he went for food. She ate when he told her to, the canopy still not ready. And when he said, "Let me do it for a few minutes,

Iris," she wanted to rage at something. Someone. Anyone. Anything.

"I'll be back in a minute," she said through clenched teeth. She walked away, her feet sinking into the looser sand along the tree line. When she was far enough away, she sank against a tree and let her tears come.

She wasn't even sure what she was so upset about. She'd been the one who wanted to wait until day seven. Something had shifted though, while she looked at those stars, and she needed to get off this island.

Her mind wandered, and she wondered where she and Justin would be had he not hauled her over the side of the ship and into that lifeboat. She knew these were dangerous waters for her thoughts, but she let them swim around anyway, gaining momentum, until they had a whirlpool going in her brain.

It was *his* fault they were out here. Everyone else was probably safe in Getaway Bay, rebooked onto a different cruise. And she'd been eating rambutan and dragon fruit for three days with sand everywhere, and very little drinking water. Honestly, if she never saw another piece of fruit again, she'd die happy.

Her stomach cramped at the thought, and she wiped her eyes. Crying wouldn't get her anywhere. It hadn't when Eden was stranded up on the mountain. It hadn't when her father had been diagnosed with cancer. It hadn't when Orchid's husband had died.

She'd been through hard things before. She could do this too.

You can do this, she told herself as she stood up and brushed sand from her shorts.

Back at the shelter, Justin wrestled with the fronds, a look of pure determination drawing down his eyebrows. "How's it going?" she asked, somewhat relieved they were giving him as much trouble as they did her.

"I had to go back a bit," he said. "I think if it's a little longer, we can pull it tighter and have a better grip." He wove faster than she did, and she decided not to take it personally. Soon enough, he stood up and glanced at her. "Let's go try it."

She went with him down the beach, and positioned herself in the boat the way she had before. He moved to the back, because he was taller and could reach the tops of the poles even though the boat was slanted down.

"You put yours in," he said, and she fitted the poles through the holes in the palm fronds he'd made.

"Okay," she said, thinking they were getting a lot of practice doing things they probably wouldn't have to do until they were married. She wasn't sure what she thought of that, but she was pretty sure she could handle putting together an entertainment center with him after this.

"I'm going to pull hard," he said. "You push against the poles, okay?"

"Okay." She braced one had against each pole and

pushed. He pulled, and he was so much stronger than her that the poles still bent. "They're bending."

"It's okay," he said. "That'll make it tighter when I let go." He grunted behind her, and then he said, "Got it. You can let go."

She did and carefully ducked under the canopy and stepped out of the boat. "This is only going to give us shade when the sun is directly overhead," she said, wishing she'd thought of it before.

"I'm going to use the emergency blanket as a shield," he said. "We can move it wherever we need to."

"Oh, okay." Foolishness hit her, and she wanted to cry again. She wasn't even sure why. She was grateful Justin was there with her, doing some of the hard work.

He stretched his back and looked up into the sky. "Let's load the food."

She helped him carry all the fruit they'd gathered to the boat. It was easily enough for a few days, and if she had to live on that boat with him that long, Iris wasn't sure what she'd do. But she knew being on the water wasn't as easy as living on the island, and she hoped he was right in saying they'd only be confined to the boat for twenty-four hours.

Iris collected the water filtration system while Justin brought down the drinking water they'd collected. "We should drink this now," she said. "I don't think it's going to make it over the break."

"Probably not," he said, and he lifted one of the

coconut shells to his lips. She drank as much as she dared to, and then she climbed in the boat, sitting where Justin told her to.

"Ready?" he asked.

She nodded, sending up another prayer to whoever was listening. Justin pushed them into the water, and jumped into the boat, splashing warm water on her legs.

"Here we go," he said, setting his hands on the oars. She wished he didn't sound quite so fatalistic, but as he rowed out into the waves, she understood why.

It would be a freaking miracle if they got over this break without capsizing, losing all their food, and busting up their boat.

A complete miracle.

CHAPTER TEN

Justin refused to focus further than ten feet in front of him. He didn't want to see the way the waves crashed over the break, couldn't stand to let himself doubt that they couldn't get away from this island.

Guilt pulled through him with the sharpness of a fishhook, and he had to make things right. He had to get them back to civilization.

He pulled against the water, wishing it would just relax for one minute. Sixty seconds. Then he could get them over the break and back out into the open ocean. He'd have to row a lot to get them back where they needed to be, but he could do it.

Sure, his muscles burned already, and the four days without adequate nutrition certainly wasn't helping. But he was going to do this. He'd been in difficult and trying situations before. He'd spent two days in a hole in the desert, for crying out loud. He'd spent sixty hours confined in a submarine.

He could get them over this break and back to Maui. He could, and he would. Justin had a mental space where he went when things were tough as a SEAL. He just needed to get inside that space, and he'd be fine.

So he only looked ten feet in front of him. He took each swell as it came, and he ignored the pain in his shoulders and arms. There would be time for pain later. Right now, he needed to get them over the break.

"Get in the bottom of the boat," he commanded when he saw the whitewater ahead. The break. "Now."

Thankfully, Iris didn't contradict him. Didn't argue. She just got down. She held onto two of their coconuts and steadied herself in the boat. He dug his feet into the bench in front of him, using every ounce of strength he had.

"One time," he grunted. He would get them over the very first time. If he didn't…well, he wasn't sure he had the strength to try again.

The water pushed him back violently, and he stroked against it, coming up to the break before the next wave. Halfway there, the waves pounded the boat back again. He groaned as he strained against an ocean full of water, but he could see paradise just on the other side of the break.

Three more strokes. Then two. Then one.

He made them quickly, pulling, pulling, pulling them over and into the open water.

Relief hit him, and Iris said, "Justin, you're a beast," but he didn't stop. The waves were still coming, and he didn't need them shoved back into the rocks and getting their boat smashed to smithereens.

He yanked on one side, putting the boat parallel to the break and he rowed as quickly as he could. He didn't realize how much noise he was making until Iris said, "We're clear, Justin."

"We're not," he said, still desperate to get farther from the break. "Those waves can take us right back to it."

"But we won't go over."

"We could lose our boat," he said, still positioning the boat where he wanted it. He pulled again, and then again, until he was satisfied they wouldn't be taken back to the break and get smashed up.

He relaxed, his fingers tight on the oars. He uncurled them, letting the pain flow through him now.

"Did I keep us pretty much straight out?" He needed a drink, but he didn't dare ask for one quite yet. Twisting, he looked over his shoulder to see the island behind him. Their beach was more or less right behind him, and he glanced up at the sun. It was after noon, as the sun was off to his right—to the west.

"So I'll keep the boat moving south," he said, ducking back under the palm frond canopy. "The sun needs to stay on our right. That's west."

"And at night?" she asked.

"We keep moving away from the north star." He said it so confidently, but it had been a while since Justin had had to use the stars to navigate. Even then, it had been a training mission, years ago. Over a decade.

The boats and subs the SEALs used were equipped with all the latest technology to help them navigate to within inches of their targets.

But he didn't say any of that.

He was the one who'd jumped off that cruise ship, maybe a bit prematurely, despite what the captain had said. And Justin was going to get them back to safety.

By nightfall, their drinking water was gone. The sun wasn't out to evaporate more, but Justin leaned over the side of the boat and filled the filtration bag anyway. Then, as soon as the orb came up in the morning, they could be making water.

He settled back in the boat next to Iris, who hadn't said much for the last several hours. Feeling humble and foolish, he put his arm around her. "I'm sorry I got us into this mess."

She looked up at him, and in the last rays of light, he saw that she had indeed blamed him for their tropical island adventure. But hadn't she said she thought it was romantic about those people who'd gotten stranded and fallen in love?

She had, but Justin knew they weren't in love. He leaned down and kissed her anyway, and she let him.

Seemed to enjoy it. She tucked herself into his arms and said nothing.

He didn't like it. The usually chatty Iris surely had something to say. But she remained silent, so he decided he could talk.

"Remember how I told you about Heath? Well, one time, he was manning our rig, and a storm came up. The Indian Ocean can be cruel, though I suppose they all can be." He gazed at the undulating water, keeping one hand on the oar on his right. He had the urge to check the stars every few seconds, but he refrained.

The white tips of the water encouraged him to keep talking. "Anyway, before we knew it, we were in the midst of the squall. He had everyone hunker down, and as engine after engine went out, we thought that was it for us."

He chuckled, and Iris looked up at him. "I wasn't laughing then," he said. "But Heath did some crazy stuff. And he didn't hesitate. He just acted. He gave orders. We followed them." Justin was almost desperate for her to understand. "That's why I grabbed you and took you overboard with me," he said. "I really thought that cruise ship was going down."

"I know," she said, her voice deathly quiet in the night surrounding them.

"I'm sorry," he said. "The captain said to evacuate. I mean, I have hearing aids, and they were turned down, but I heard him."

"It's okay," she said, stretching up to kiss him.

Justin took his time, exploring her mouth completely before pulling away.

"You have hearing aids?" Iris asked, her lips catching on his.

"Just keep an eye on the stars. I can keep us going in the right direction in the morning so you can sleep."

"Okay," Justin agreed, but he knew one thing. He would not be sleeping until they were back on a populated island.

THE NIGHT PASSED, AND JUSTIN ADJUSTED THE foily emergency blanket to keep the sun off their east side. He felt sure they'd get somewhere in only another hour.

Then another.

Then another.

Hopelessness filled him, choking off his vocal cords. He couldn't help the path his thoughts took, and that was down the same trail that had kept him single all this time. His job had been too dangerous for a family before.

But maybe it was *him* that was the curse.

He made Iris drink as much as he dared, until she realized what he was doing. "You have to drink too," she said, wiping her hair off her forehead.

"I'm fine," he said.

"Justin." She shook the cup toward him. "You really

have to. I can't row us to an island, and I don't need you passing out from dehydration trying to do it."

He looked at her miserably, trying to glare but too thirsty to do it. He took the cup and drank the rest of the water, filled up the bag and set it on the stern so the sun could start baking it—the way it was baking him.

"I'm sorry," he said, though it wasn't the first time.

Iris gave him a smile that didn't exactly say *it's okay* and turned back to the front of the boat. "I'm sure we'll be there soon."

Justin wanted to agree with her, but he was starting to doubt they'd ever get somewhere safe. Maybe they should've stayed on the island. Maybe he could've learned to like eating fruit for every meal.

Maybe he shouldn't have leapt off that cruise ship quite so fast.

The sun arced across the sky, and he moved the emergency blanket to the other side of the boat, wondering why he'd liked Hawaii so much previous to now. The sun was brutal, and relentless, and he blinked and he swore he saw land ahead.

"Is that...?" He didn't dare finish his question, because he didn't want to be wrong. Again.

Iris didn't stir, and alarm pulled through him. "Iris?"

She groaned, and Justin left the oars for a moment to check on her. She'd curled up in the bottom of the boat between the seats in front of him, and he bent over. "Iris? You okay?" He wanted to add *sweetheart*, but he didn't need to add more emotion than necessary.

Her eyes fluttered and opened, and she nodded. "I'm just tired."

He didn't see how that was possible, but he went back to his place, made sure they were still moving south, and started praying.

Night started to fall, and Justin didn't dare blink. He'd seen a light in the distance, he was sure of it. "Iris," he said again, but she didn't move. The sun sank completely, leaving them in dim twilight, and there were definitely lights ahead.

"Iris," he barked. "There's land ahead." It was hard for him to tell how far away it was, especially the way his head swam around like it had been dunked in the ocean.

"I'm going to have to take us over the break in the dark," he said, true fear coming into his voice and mind and heart. "Iris, I need your help."

She still didn't move, and Justin really wanted to share his relief with her. "Iris." He leaned over to check on her again, and she looked passed out.

Because she was.

"Iris." Justin leapt over the seat as quickly as he could, knocking his head against the woven canopy they didn't need anymore. "Iris? Sweetheart, I need you to wake up."

He cradled her in his arms, the heat from her skin

far too warm. He didn't understand. She'd eaten fruit all day. Drank most of the water. Stayed out of the sun.

"Iris," he said again, so tired of saying her name. "We're almost there, sweetheart. I need your help to get across the break."

Still, she didn't stir.

Justin didn't know what to do.

Focus.

Get the job done.

Complete the mission.

And he needed to get them over the break and to solid ground. Then he could call for help.

In fact, he might be able to call for help right now. He went back to his spot in the boat and pulled his phone out of Iris's hip pack. It seemed to take forever to power up, and when it did, he had two bars of service.

He swiped and tapped three numbers, so many emotions flowing through him it was very hard to focus.

CHAPTER ELEVEN

Iris didn't like the blackness in her mind. She couldn't seem to shake it off, though, even when someone kept calling her name. She seemed to be moving, and then a man was talking again. Saying all kinds of things about a deserted island and being in a boat for over twenty-four hours.

She swam closer to the surface, finally breaking through right when the man stopped talking. Iris groaned, and someone said, "Iris? Can you wake up?"

Justin's face appeared above her, and everything inside her burned. Her head ached, and sharp pain moved through her neck.

"We're almost back," he said. "I need your help. Can you sit up?"

She sure liked hearing him say he needed her help, but she couldn't manage to get herself sitting up. He moved around the boat, jostling her from side to side, as he took down the canopy. "I called nine-one-one, and they're going to send emergency vehicles to the three ports on this side of the island."

One corner, then the next, and the wide sky gaped open above her. Iris wanted to flinch away from it, go back to sleep.

"I'm going to try to wait to go over the break until we see one. Then we can get to it easier."

Iris wasn't sure what he was saying. She managed to get upright and press her back into the seat behind her. "What?"

"I need your help to find the emergency vehicles. And to get over the break. We won't be able to see it until we're nearly on it, and that'll be when I need to row the most."

He finished taking down the canopy and sat in his spot beside the oars. Iris looked ahead, finally realizing what was going on. "Justin, there are lights up there."

"I know," he said. "We made it back to Maui."

She twisted to find him smiling. "We made it back to Maui. How long have I been asleep?"

"I don't know," he said, nodding to his left. "I see some red flashing lights over there. Do you think that's the closest place?"

Iris turned too quickly, and vertigo overcame her. "Whoa," she said, covering her face with both of her hands. The spinning finally stopped, and she dared to look toward the island again.

"I don't see any other lights," she said, her voice weary.

"I'm going to get us back," he said.

"Seems that way," Iris said. A bright white light streamed out from a spot just to their right. "But that's closer."

"That's a boat," Justin said, making an adjustment. "Maybe we won't have to go over the break." He stopped rowing completely, and Iris felt like she was going to be sick.

In fact, she scrambled for the edge of the boat so she could throw up over the side. After she finished, she hung onto the boat and moaned. "I don't feel so great."

"You're sick," he said. "I'm so, so sorry, Iris. Just hang on a little longer."

Hang on, she did. The boat definitely came closer, and Justin just let the waves push and pull them wherever they wanted to. He turned the flashlight on his phone and lifted it above his head, waving it slowly back and forth in a wide arc.

"Vessel ahead, this is Maui Harbor Police," a man said over the intercom as the boat came closer. "Identify yourselves."

"We need help," Justin yelled, causing Iris to flinch away from the noise.

"Please stay there," the man said, and within a couple of minutes, a smaller boat headed toward them.

Relief filled Iris, and she hoped she'd never have to see or eat another piece of dragon fruit again.

"Take her," Justin said. "She's not well. Temperature over a hundred degrees. Neither of us have had enough water, and we've been eating only fruit for days."

"Ma'am? Can you tell me your name?"

Iris blinked at the man on the other boat. Wow, they'd gotten here fast. "Iris…."

"Just take her," Justin snapped. "Her name is Iris McLaughlin. She just threw up, and she needs fluids, food, meds."

Iris turned her head toward him, but every moment felt so slow, as if she were moving under quicksand.

Justin pulled his arm away from the man trying to help him. "Get her off this boat. I am Commander Justin Brunner, Navy SEAL Delivery Vehicle Team One. I'm fine. *She* needs help."

Iris tried to stand up, but everything beneath her swayed. She lurched, and someone grabbed her arm. A man kept asking her questions, but she didn't have the energy or mental power to respond.

Justin was talking, and he'd tell them everything they needed to know. On the bigger boat, Iris let the people take her wherever they wanted, and she made it to an office before she passed out.

WHEN SHE WOKE UP NEXT, THE FIRST THING she heard was Ivy's voice. "...I mean, can you believe that?"

Eden's lower tone chimed in, but Iris couldn't make out the words. She opened her eyes, and she saw her sisters huddled together several feet away. The steady beeping and horrible fluorescent lighting testified that she was in the hospital.

"Aunt Iris," her niece said, and everyone swung their attention toward the bed.

"Heya, Tesla," Iris croaked. Her throat felt like someone had packed it with wet sand, and she coughed.

"You're awake," Eden said at the same time Ivy squealed and launched herself at the bed. She let her sister cry, Ivy's tears wetting Iris's face. "We had no idea where you were," she said. "No idea. The rescue boats came back day after day with nothing."

"Ivy," Orchid said, nudging her back. "She's fine."

"She's not fine," Ivy said, her blue eyes flashing in a familiar way. "She fainted once she got off that boat, and she's been asleep for hours."

"I'm fine," Iris said, trying to push herself up. She didn't quite have the strength and stopped trying. "Where's Justin?"

"Who?" Ivy asked.

"He's not here," Eden said. "He wasn't nearly as... sick as you. They checked him out and he left."

"He left?" Iris looked at Eden, so many questions running through her mind. "Where are we?"

"Maui," her mother said. "We came as soon as the cruise line notified us that you weren't on board."

Iris wanted to know everything that had happened after she and Justin had jumped off that cruise ship, so she said, "Tell me about it," and listened as the story got told by everyone, each saying a line or two, contradicting each other, and bickering until it was all out.

Yes, she and Justin were the only people unaccounted for on the lame boat. It had limped back to the port in Maui after the whale attacks before anyone noticed they weren't there.

Calls had been made. A new boat sent. The Coast Guard and Maui Harbor Patrol notified. Her family had come immediately, and several of Justin's friends.

"You have got to introduce me to some of them," Ivy said with a toss of her blonde hair. "Did you know Navy SEALs are called Frogmen? I've been messaging my Frogman, but he hasn't responded."

Iris, buoyed up by the energy of her family, looked at Ivy, almost afraid to tell her. "I know who he is."

"Yeah, who?" Ivy leaned forward. "Because not a single one of his friends will admit to even being on Getaway Bay Singles. But that can't be true, can it?" Ivy leaned forward, and Iris couldn't believe this was the conversation she was having in the hospital after being stranded on an island for days.

"It's Justin," she said.

For once, her family remained silent for several seconds. Then Eden started laughing, and it didn't take long for Orchid to join in.

"The guy she was stranded with," Eden said, getting right in Ivy's face. "I don't think Frogman is going to be calling you back."

"You don't call on the app," Ivy said, rolling her eyes. "And why wouldn't he message me back?"

"It's obvious," Eden said, casting a look over her shoulder. "He and Iris have a thing."

"No," Iris said, not wanting to hurt her twin sister. "He's just the meathead who grabbed me and made me jump off that boat."

"Oh, she's still a bad liar," Orchid said as a nurse came in. "Come on, sweetie. Let's leave Auntie Iris alone for a few minutes."

Everyone started to leave as the nurse checked monitors. Ivy stayed, her eyes searching Iris's. "Tell me the truth, at least," she said, glancing at the nurse. "He hasn't come to see you, and you've been asleep for fifteen hours."

Iris tried not to let that information hurt her, but it stung way down deep in her lungs. She didn't have her phone, or even Justin's number. How could she get him to come see her? Why hadn't he?

She looked up into Ivy's eyes, and said, "It was nothing."

Ivy nodded, always so trusting when it came to twin stuff, and started toward the door. "I'll go get you some chocolate pie. It's actually pretty good here." She smiled and left, and Iris faced the nurse.

"How bad is it?" she asked.

"You're doing great," she said, smiling. "Any pain? Headache?"

"No," Iris said. "I feel pretty good."

"We need to get the catheter out, and the doctor will need to come check you before you can go." She made a note on her chart and leaned forward, her dark eyes sparkling. "And just so you know, there *was* a man here really early this morning before the sun even came up. Big guy. Shaved hair. Tattoos. He held your hand and kept his forehead right there against the rail, murmuring to himself."

She tapped the clipboard against the rail. "Looked like he cared about you to me." With a quick smile, she left the room too. Left Iris to stew over what she'd said and if Justin had really come to see her in the pre-dawn hours.

By the time she got out of the hospital, night had fallen again, and her parents had booked a couple of rooms at a hotel on the island until they could get back to Getaway Bay.

"I brought you some clothes," Ivy said, bouncing on the bed in the hotel room the twins would be sharing.

"Did someone get my hip pack?" she asked.

"No," Ivy said. "Why?"

"My phone was in there." Iris hadn't been able to use it out on the tiny island, but now that she was in a more civilized place, she wanted to use it. Check in with her employees.

Maybe figure out a way to get in touch with Justin.

Iris was a little surprised at how much she missed him. She'd never particularly liked being alone, and with Ivy, she never really had been by herself. But she didn't crave being surrounded by her friends at work, nor her family.

She wanted to know how Justin was, and who had come to meet him in Maui, and why he hadn't wanted to come visit her while her family was in the room.

Ivy made hot chocolate and turned on a movie, and the twins curled up together on the same bed. About halfway through the movie, a knock sounded on the door, and Ivy went to get it.

Iris expected to see Tesla or Orchid, maybe even Eden. Instead, Ivy stayed at the door, having a conversation, and then she came back into the room alone. She held up Iris's phone. "That was the guy from the front desk. He said someone left this for you."

Iris reached for it even as surprise moved through her. Justin. How had he known where she was? And why didn't he just bring it up himself?

Iris was going to find out.

CHAPTER TWELVE

Justin walked away from the hotel where Iris was staying with her family, his mood melancholy. Surely she had to know he'd brought the phone back, and as soon as she got it, he wondered what she'd do.

He hadn't given her his number. She couldn't call.

"Did she get it?" Heath asked, clapping Justin on the shoulder as he joined him on the curb across the street.

"I'm assuming."

"Why don't you just go talk to her?"

"I don't know, man." Justin tried to give him a smile, and Lucas stood from the bench where he'd been on the phone.

"We ready to go?"

"I don't need a helicopter ride back to Getaway Bay."

"But the Navy said we could use it." Lucas grinned at him like it would be a grand adventure, as if none of them had ever flown in a helicopter before. "So let's go home. Maui is nice and all, but it's full of tourists."

"So is Getaway Bay," Justin said, so glad his friends had come for him. He did belong somewhere.

"It's not really," Heath said. "Just a couple of spots. And it's growing a lot, with real people living there."

Justin looked at him. "So are you going to retire and stay on the island? I thought you were going back to Texas."

"Well, I'm not retiring," Heath said. "For years."

"You're maybe eighteen months out," Justin said.

"But I'm not taking retirement when I can, just because I can." Heath raised his right eyebrow at Justin. "And why aren't you married yet, man? Isn't that why you got out?"

"No," Justin said, though he *had* wanted to find someone to settle down with. "I got out, because it was time for me to get out."

"We just need to get Diego away from the waitress he met during lunch."

"Oh, boy," Justin said with a smirk. "That guy needs to find someone and settle down."

"At least he has dates," Heath said.

Justin wanted to tell them he'd just had a really long date, where he kissed a girl and held her close while they slept on a platform they'd built with their bare hands. Instead, he said nothing.

He wasn't sure how to go back to Iris. The guilt he felt ripped through him the way bombs did when they exploded on buildings. He'd put her life in danger, and he didn't want to be the reason she wasn't happy.

"He's in here," Lucas said, opening the door to an ice cream shop. A bell rang, and Justin opted to wait on the street.

Heath and Lucas went in, and Justin pulled out his phone. He hadn't cheated and taken her number from her phone. He wasn't sure why. He just knew that things felt different now, and a gulf existed between him and Iris that hadn't been there before that last night on the island.

Twenty minutes later, his SEAL buddies came out of the ice cream shop, laughing, and Justin turned toward them. "It's about time."

"Hey, she was really pretty," Diego said. "And I got her number." He singsonged the last word, wagging his phone around like the Navy player didn't get numbers every day of his life. Seriously, he went out with more women than Justin thought possible.

"And what?" Heath asked. "You're going to have a long-distance relationship? She knows you work on a different island, right?"

"There are so many ways to communicate now," Diego said. "And I get leave."

They continued to rib him as Lucas drove to the helipad. Justin didn't have a bag besides Iris's hip pack, and he wasn't sure why he hadn't given that to the guy at the front desk too. Neither one of them needed the supplies inside it, and he just wanted to hold onto it a little longer.

He knew why, even if he hadn't admitted it yet. That hip pack was his only remaining connection to Iris.

THE NEXT MORNING, HE WOKE UP IN HIS OWN bed, his back aching and his neck stiff. He had no idea why, other than his misery had followed him back to his apartment.

He sat up, a groan coming from his mouth as he rubbed his neck. His phone flashed with a green light, which mean a notification from one of his social media apps. Probably no one he wanted to talk to, but he swiped the device on anyway.

Getaway Bay Singles.

Iris's sister had messaged him several times, but he hadn't chatted her back. Surely Iris would tell her twin who he was, and what…they were. But he didn't even know what they were, so maybe she hadn't.

And this message wasn't from PoisonedApple, but a potential connection request from a woman named DragonFruit.

His heart leapt to the back of his throat as he tapped on the name.

Hey, Frogman. I heard you were back in town. When I get

back, maybe we could have dinner? There will be no dragon fruit or rambutans.

Justin really wanted to say yes. He even chuckled at her promise of no fruit for dinner.

But he decided to be honest.

I don't know, he messaged back, checking the time stamp on her message. It had come last night, probably while he was flying back over the ocean to Getaway Bay, his buddies' laughter in his headset.

He exhaled, trying to reason through the confusing thoughts in his head. It was impossible. *I'm worried we're not a good fit.*

He stared at the words, because they weren't quite right. He liked Iris a whole lot. She was strong, and capable, and beautiful, and she kissed him in a way that made him feel whole in a world where he'd always been just a little less than that.

He erased the sentence, trying to find a better one.

What don't you know? popped up on his screen before he could.

I need some time, he said, sending that before he could second-guess himself.

Time for what?

Iris was going to be relentless, he could tell. And it was something he really liked about her. He looked up from his phone, knowing that she'd done a lot for him on that island. Maybe she couldn't scale the banana tree or open the coconut, but she'd helped him see himself in a new way. Helped him clarify what he really wanted out of life.

Time to figure out if I'm good for you or not. He sent the message and got up to pace. He moved to the window and back to the bed, the flashing green light already back on his phone.

Why do you get to decide that?

He's just the meathead who grabbed me and made me jump off that boat.

Her words to her family echoed through his mind. He'd been about to go into the room, right behind the nurse. Announce himself. He'd already been to see her that morning, and her vitals looked good. Her color was better. The nurse had assured him she'd likely make a full recovery.

Because you need time to figure out if I'm good for you or not.

Iris didn't respond immediately, and he knew he'd spoken true. Messaged true. Whatever. The point was, she did blame him for dragging her off that boat and condemning her to an island life for a few days. And the fact was, she had gotten very ill on the way back, and if something had happened to her....

Justin blew out his breath. He knew better than to play the what-if game, and he pushed the thoughts away now too.

His phone rang next, and his heart hammered in anticipation. "Can't be Iris," he muttered, and sure enough the screen had Theo's name on it.

"Hey, boss," Justin said, trying to infuse some enthusiasm into his voice. He did too good of a job, because he sounded absolutely delighted to have his boss calling him. "Am I late?"

"It's not even seven yet," Theo said.

"Right." Justin paced over to the window and looked out. The sun was coming up, the same, relentless way it did every day. He turned away from the golden light, which he usually found so comforting.

His stomach growled as Theo said, "You're not coming in today."

"Okay," Justin said.

"Wow," Theo said. "I was expecting that to be harder."

"When do you need me back by?"

"Well, I've assigned Cruise Hawaii to someone else, and I think you were on the Umbrella Project next, and we're weeks from that."

"Weeks." Justin didn't want to be alone for weeks. But he easily could be. He could leave the island, and no one would know. He could stay right here in this apartment, and never shower, and never leave, and one day someone might smell something and come knocking.

Misery wept through him, and he sighed. "I'll be in tomorrow. Think you could give me something to do?"

"Absolutely," Theo said. "But only if you're up to it."

"I have to…have something to do." A reason to get up and get out of the house. But he didn't say that.

"I'll have food at the office tomorrow."

"Thanks, Theo." The call ended, and Justin decided he would not be spending the day inside this apartment. He wanted to eat as much as he could—bacon, eggs, turkey sandwiches, chicken fried steak, French fries. All of it. And then he was going to figure out what to do with his life.

He did just that, walking down the boardwalk between East Bay and Getaway Bay with tacos in his hand once and then a smoothie the next time. The trees kept the boardwalk between the two bays shaded, and he liked watching the people who'd come to the island for vacation, as well as the locals who came to this section of the beach to eat.

The day passed before he got another message from DragonFruit. *Why wouldn't you be good for me?*

A flash of annoyance and anger ran through him. *Maybe because I'm a meathead who made you jump off the boat.*

As soon as he sent the message, he regretted it. But it was done now, and the Getaway Bay Singles app told him when she'd read it.

And she had. Nothing he could do to take it back now.

CHAPTER THIRTEEN

*I*ris blinked at her screen, pure alarm ringing through her. *Maybe because I'm a meathead who made you jump off the boat.*

He'd heard her. She'd said that her family, yesterday morning in the hospital on Maui. *He'd heard her.*

Regret lanced through her, even as another message from him came in. *I was trying to save you, by the way. I'm not perfect, and I've apologized a bunch of times.*

She'd never said he hadn't apologized, nor had she ever accused him of being perfect—though he was pretty darn close to that. And she may have put some blame on him on the island, gone through a rough time where she thought maybe they wouldn't be able to get off the island, maybe thought he was a little barky sometimes. Thought things should be done his way.

But when he'd pulled rank on those officers with the Maui Harbor Police, Iris had wanted to kiss him.

"I shouldn't have said that," she said out loud, typing the words into the dating app. She hated with every fiber of her being that she had to communicate with him this way. There was so much going on in the hospital room, and she'd seen the look on Ivy's face, and Eden's, and her mom's, and she'd said it.

She sent the first message and quickly added, *Can I call you?*

I'm tired, he sent back. Maybe tomorrow.

Tomorrow came, and with it all the regular frustration of Iris's life. She hadn't gotten her two weeks of blissful vacation, and when she walked into We'll Weed That at eight a.m. the next day, the receptionist rose from her desk like she was seeing the dead.

"Iris," she said, one hand going to her mouth. "What are you doing here?"

"I own this company," she said, hating the way her high heels clicked against the floor. She'd used to love that. Loved her power suits on office days. Loved getting her hands dirty on outside days. Loved sitting down with her project managers and watching a yard or an outdoor space come to life.

A longing for what she'd once had radiated through her. She had no idea what it was directed at, though, and no way to go back in time and get it.

The morning passed with her reassuring everyone that she was fine. Yes, she could work. Sure, send over the phone call.

She left by lunch, utterly exhausted. The doctor had

told her to take it easy for a few days, but Iris couldn't stand to be idle for long. And being alone with her thoughts was an exquisite sort of torture she did not want to endure.

Her first instinct was to call Justin and ask him if he was working. Maybe they could grab a drink and watch the waves come in. But that sort of date held very little romance for Iris anymore. She'd seen enough waves come in to last a lifetime.

So she got her own drink from Two Coconuts and went home. Ivy had been there, as evidenced by the fresh loaf of bread sitting on Iris's countertop. "Mom and I made this. Call me when you get home."

Ivy would come over if Iris asked, and she suddenly needed to talk through everything with her sister.

"Hey," she said when Ivy picked up. "When are you off?" Her twin worked as a retail manager at a boutique downtown, and she had a flexible schedule.

"It's so slow today," she said. "We just need to wait for Twitchy to show up, and I can come over."

Iris liked how she said "we," as if she and Iris were still a team. They had been their whole lives, and Iris wished she'd just told Ivy the truth in the hospital yesterday.

She buttered bread and ate it, changed into her yoga pants, and had just started to doze on the couch when Ivy showed up. She'd brought Indian food from The Indian House, and the scent of butter chicken made Iris's mouth water.

"You're a lifesaver," she said, hugging her twin with a fierceness that made her throat close with emotion.

"You said you never wanted to eat fruit again," Ivy said, holding Iris tight too. "And you've seriously lost fifteen pounds."

Iris didn't argue even though it wasn't true. She stepped back and accepted the container of food before putting it on a plate and taking it to the couch. Ivy joined her, tucking her feet under her before digging into the chicken and rice.

"I have to tell you something," Iris said, pushing her food around inside the Styrofoam container.

"Yeah?" Ivy finished chewing and swallowed. "Work? Man? Island?"

"Island," Iris said. "And man."

Ivy paused, and their eyes met. "So it's about Justin."

Iris nodded. "We sort of connected out there." She shrugged, trying to make it seem like no big deal. But it was a big deal, and she hated that she'd just tried to downplay their relationship again. "I met him on the cruise, obviously, before the whales attacked. He was a little...Navy SEAL."

Ivy played the perfect twin, listening to Iris's story and nodding in all the right places. When Iris said, "And we kissed, and it was magical and wonderful, and so hot all at the same time."

She paused, hoping Ivy would tell her what to do

now. "So you didn't want to tell me, because you thought I'd be upset."

"He was yours first," Iris said. "And you've always hated me for coming in and stealing guys from you."

"So you're admitting you did that with Jake."

"We were fifteen."

"You've never admitted it, Iris."

And she didn't want to now. But she desperately didn't want this guilt either, and she did want Justin.

She opened her mouth to speak, realizing what she'd just thought.

She wanted Justin.

"Yes," she said. "Okay? I stole him from you when we were teenagers. But this wasn't that, I swear."

Ivy pursed her lips and said, "Mm hm," as she scooped up another bite of chicken and rice.

"It wasn't. I didn't even know you two had a thing until we'd been on the island for a day or two." Or shorter. Longer? Iris couldn't even think of how long she and Justin had been out there. Had it really only been a few days?

Ivy held onto her anger for another moment. "It's fine," she said. "I was flirting with him pretty hard, and he never asked me out."

"He said he probably would've, eventually." Iris watched her sister's face, watched the annoyance roll through her eyes.

"I don't want eventually," she said. "You can have him."

"I wish," Iris said, looking down at her mostly full plate. "He overheard me call him a meathead who made me jump off the boat."

Ivy sucked in a breath, her eyes going wide. "That's not good."

"He already feels guilty for doing it, and I knew that. I just…I'd just woken up, and Eden was looking at me like I'd gone and fallen in love with him, the way she did Holden."

"Her and Holden were always going to get back together," Ivy said. "It just took an act of God to make it happen. Finally."

Iris agreed, and she wondered if this was an act of God to put a man in her life she would've bypassed initially. Not even considered. Warned her sister away from dating.

And why? Because he had a loud bark and a few tattoos?

His tattoos were sexy, and Iris could deal with bark, because she also knew what he was like in his most vulnerable moments. Right before he fell asleep and right after he woke up. When he was hungry, and desperate, and pulling with everything he had to save them.

"Iris," her sister said, and Iris pulled herself from her thoughts.

"Hmm?"

"You haven't heard a word I've said." Ivy had put

her plate down and everything. She got up and took Iris's from her. "You like him, right?"

Iris nodded, her chest tightening. "He said he needed time to figure out if he was good for me." Her heart shriveled up inside her, and she looked at her sister with watery eyes.

"Oh, honey, you fell in love with him." Ivy stared at her, searching her face for the truth.

"No." Iris sniffed and wiped her eyes before any tears leaked out. "I'm not Orchid. I didn't fall in love at first sight. In fact, he was kind of rude the first time I met him."

Ivy giggled, which caused Iris to giggle, and pretty soon they were both laughing. Ivy sobered first, and she said, "But you did."

"I didn't," Iris insisted. "Eden's the one who holds out on kissing a guy until she's like, two breaths from falling in love with him. I can kiss and still be in like."

Ivy cocked her head and waited.

"What?" Iris asked. "Honestly, Ivy. I'm not in love with him. We've only known each other for a few days."

"And you went through some very significant things during those *six* days," she said.

"I asked him to dinner, and he said no. He won't give me his phone number."

"How are you talking to him?"

"I had to join that singles app."

Ivy blinked and then burst out laughing. "Oh,

honey, if you can't see you love him just because of that...." She shook her head. "I can't help you."

"But I need help." Iris must've infused the right amount of desperation and whine in her voice, because Ivy looked sympathetic.

"Look," she said, getting up to take the plates back into the kitchen. "You're smart. I can tell you all kinds of things to do. Like, why was he on the cruise? Could you get him out on another one, and just happen to be there? Where does he work? Could you hire him somehow, and show up and be like, hey, what are the chances?" She tossed her hair like she was a professional matchmaker.

And honestly, she should be, because both of the things she'd just said would totally work. She knew where Justin spent his time during the day. He built apps—and We'll Weed That did not have an app.

Yet.

And he'd been on that cruise as research for another project. So she could call his boss and find out when the replacement cruise would be happening. Problems sprang to her mind—maybe his boss would send someone else to do the research. Maybe projects couldn't just be assigned to whoever she wanted them to—but she ignored them.

"Ivy, you've got real game," she said.

"I know," Ivy said, rolling her eyes. "It's why I've been out with every eligible bachelor on this island." She grinned at Iris. "Hey, maybe I should try going on a cruise." She lifted her eyebrows rapidly a few times. "Find me a single Navy SEAL."

"I wouldn't," Iris said. "It was mostly couples and families on that thing."

Ivy sighed, a long, happy sigh Iris had heard her sister utter after so many dates growing up.

"What?" she asked.

"Then it was fate you two met."

Iris rolled her eyes now, because Ivy had always tended to over-romanticize things. But her mind seized onto that word, and she couldn't help thinking that maybe it was fate that they were on that same cruise, at the same time.

"Yeah," she muttered as her twin looked for a romantic comedy that was "sure to cheer her up."

"And maybe he was with you so you didn't die." Even if he had grabbed onto her and jumped into the lifeboat with her.

So now, she just needed to figure out how to get back in the game with Justin. Ivy had listed a couple of great ideas….

"You really don't need to give Cruise Hawaii to someone else," Justin said. Theo stood behind three monitors, while his partner, Ben, pointed to a fourth.

Justin felt like he'd been talking to a brick wall for the past ten minutes. But he couldn't survive another day like yesterday, where he just wandered around and did nothing. Sure, he'd enjoyed the food. Theo had brought in a full bagel and fruit bar this morning. Justin hadn't touched a single piece of fruit, and his stomach hurt from the copious amounts of carbs and cream cheese he'd consumed.

He was drinking fruit, as Getaway Bay really had some of the best smoothies on the planet.

"Theo," he said, about to slip into his Navy SEAL voice. The man finally looked over the top of the monitors. "I have nothing to do, and I'm going to lose my fricking mind." He lifted his eyebrows, hoping the message got through. "I can work on Cruise Hawaii."

Theo glanced at Ben and came around to the front of the desk. "You want to go on another cruise?"

"There was a freak accident," Justin said. "The boat didn't sink, though I thought it was going to." He was trained to assess and act. He did both things quickly, and in this case, a little too quickly.

So he'd slow down next time.

Plus, there wasn't going to be a next time. The company had issued statement after statement that they'd never lost a boat at sea, and that record was still true. The cruises were safe. He felt bad he'd caused so many problems for so many people by prematurely abandoning ship, despite what the captain had said.

"I can go back out," he said.

"Look at the schedule, Ben," Theo said, and Ben started scrolling on his phone.

"The schedule should definitely be the first thing you see on the app," he said. "Their website is awful too. How did we book last time?"

"Had to call," Theo said, folding his arms. "How's the web redesign coming? Maybe you could work on that."

"We got two new inquiries this morning too," Ben said without looking up from his phone. "A landscaping place, and a dog salon."

"There you go," Theo said. "And you're ready to take a project from inquiry to completion, Justin."

"Am I?"

"Sure," Theo said. "It would be good for you."

"Yes, hi," Ben said, stepping away to talk to the people at Cruise Hawaii.

Justin felt a measure of pride move through him. He'd only been working at The Web Developer for a year, and he'd admitted it could be boring. But taking on more of an active role? He'd love that.

"Okay," he said. "But I do want to take the cruise. I need a vacation." He smiled, glad he wasn't stuck at home or desperate to fill the hours.

"Next one isn't until next week," Ben said, tilting the phone away from his mouth.

"Okay," Justin said, and Ben went back to booking it. "And I can start on one of the new inquiries in the meantime."

"Fine," Theo said with a smile. "I want Reuben coaching you on it."

"That's great," Justin said. He got along fine with Reuben. "Which one is he doing?"

"Ben'll know."

Sure enough, when Ben got off the phone with the cruise line, he said, "You're set, Justin. Monday morning, ten a.m."

"Which project did Rueben take?" Theo asked.

"Uh, let's see." More tapping and swiping on the phone. Justin swore that Ben had four brains at his disposal, and three of them were in his phone. "We'll Weed That. They do landscaping projects, simple yard work, weekly, monthly, all of it. They have a nursery too, and they want a shopping component for their app."

The air left Justin's lungs in a low hiss. He knew exactly what We'll Weed That did. And he knew exactly why they'd suddenly decided they needed a top-of-the-line app from The Web Developer.

Both Ben and Theo looked at him, extreme interest in their expressions. "What?" Ben asked, glancing at Theo. "What did I miss?"

"I have no idea," Theo said.

But it wasn't them who'd missed something. It was Justin. He didn't need to get into all the details of his relationship with Iris. He was already twenty texts behind with his SEAL buddies, and none of them understood why he hadn't gone up to the hotel room himself, why he couldn't just call Iris.

And now she'd made sure she could come to him.

Warmth filled him, and he stood up. "Nothing," he said in a very convincing voice. "I'll talk to Reuben, and we'll get started."

APPARENTLY, THERE WAS A TON OF groundwork to do before meeting with a client for a proposal and a presentation. Justin did that work, marveling at how Iris had stayed in business with her limping website and non-existent app.

Rueben helped him every step of the way, but he also knew when to take his bearded self back to his own workstation and just let Justin do his thing. He enjoyed this new challenge, the new work he hadn't known went into prepping for a client.

And not just any client.

Iris herself had called and talked to Reuben, and Justin had made sure his name stayed out of it.

"She just called again," Reuben said, arriving at Justin's desk on Friday and setting down a paper bag. The scent of hamburgers and French fries met Justin's nose, and he practically dove for the food

"Who?"

"Iris McLaughlin. She asked if you could be assigned to her project." Reuben took a bite of his crispy chicken sandwich, his eyebrows asking too many questions.

"When's the meeting?"

"Monday."

"I can't," Justin said, looking up at his project manager. "I'm going on the cruise on Monday."

"She won't be happy about that."

Justin wasn't entirely happy about it either. "What did you tell her?"

"I didn't answer, dude. She is relentless."

Rueben had no idea just how relentless, or what that even meant. A flash of the ocean waves battering the boat ran through Justin's mind. *Those* were relentless.

"Why can't I just tell her you're the team lead on this again?"

"Because," Justin said. "It's just…complicated."

"You spent several days with her on an island. Is this an issue?" Reuben dug some fries out of his own bag.

"No," Justin said. "It's not an issue. I just don't want her to know until the meeting." An idea formed in his mind. "You call her back and tell her I'm available for the project, but not for two weeks. See what she says. Promise you'll put me on it if she agrees to wait."

Reuben shook his head. "I hate playing games."

Justin did too, but this one felt necessary. This one felt like Iris was trying to crash into his house without really thinking about what she wanted. "And if she asks you why she has to wait, tell her I'm taking a cruise and am unavailable." He wasn't sure why he was testing her like this, only that his heart felt barely able to beat.

He flipped his phone over, almost expecting that green light to be there, indicating that she'd messaged. There wasn't anything flashing there. He busied himself with the food. "I'll keep picking up your dry cleaning, and hey, that new coffee place just introduced syrups." Justin looked up at Reuben, a smile on his face.

"Fine," Reuben said. "I want coconut and caramel in my coffee." He started to walk away from Justin's desk.

He called after him, "I'm gone for two weeks starting Monday." So he could get his own coffee. And Justin would know if Iris was really desperate to see him, or just playing a game of her own.

Monday morning, he packed again, this time taking care to fill Iris's hip pack with anything he might need should he find himself once again stranded on a deserted island. He filled a backpack with protein bars, bags of beef jerky, dehydrated military rations he had left over from his time in the SEALs, a length of rope, a water bottle of significant size, water purification tables, a filtration system, a flashlight with fresh batteries, tons of emergency blankets, and three knives.

If he was going overboard, he was not going to live on dragon fruit and barely filtered ocean water.

"But you're not going overboard," he told himself, realizing he'd never pack the same way again.

He arrived at Cruise Hawaii in the appointed amount of time, but he didn't wait in the outside lobby with everyone else. The woman checked him in, and said, "Come with me, sir."

"Where are we going?" he asked, scanning the room for Iris's blonde hair. Probably a stupid move, but Reuben had texted on Friday to say that Iris had agreed to the meeting in two weeks—which meant she knew Justin would be on this cruise.

"You're a VIP," she said, smiling him through the door in the back. He entered the room there to find a suited man scrambling up from his desk.

"Mister Brunner," he said, striding forward. "We're so happy to see you back with us." He shook Justin's hand, his nerves apparent. "I once again apologize for any inconvenience on your last encounter with Cruise Hawaii."

Embarrassment filled Justin. "It's fine," he muttered. The cruise line hadn't actually done anything wrong. Whales were allowed to swim in the ocean.

"Well, we're just so glad you're back with us." He turned toward a wall of windows that looked out onto the staging area with the white tent and all the chairs. Justin had sat in the first row last time. "You'll be skipping the orientation, and you can go right to your luxury suite right now, if you'd like." He looked at Justin, the hint of a question in his gaze.

"Sure," Justin said. "No buddy system this time?"

The man blinked, obviously a little stunned. "Your buddy is already here," he said, putting his plastic smile back in place. "She said you'd be expecting her. I sent her ahead to her suite."

Justin frowned. "I'm not expecting anyone."

The man chuckled nervously. "I'm afraid I don't understand."

"You and me both," Justin said, not expecting to have to have another female buddy he needed to worry about.

What if it's Iris? he thought, and he was suddenly very keen to get to his suite. "It's fine," he said. "Do you have my suite number?"

"Right here." The man scampered over to his desk and picked up the folder of information. "I just know you're going to love our cruise, Mister Brunner."

Justin smiled at him, hating how this guy was falling all over him. It was *his fault* he'd jumped off the boat, taking Iris with him. "Thank you." He took the folder and went through the door in the back. He kept his steps even and measured, slow. But he scanned the ship in front of him for any sign of the blonde he'd hoped would come meet him here.

He'd given her all the clues. Had she taken them?

His suite sat at the top of the ship this time, and he wondered why he'd thought he'd gotten "preferential treatment" the first time. The room his keycard allowed him to enter was easily three times bigger than the one on the first level of the ship, and the bed would certainly accommodate the width of his shoulders just fine.

He put his bags down and moved to the window in the suite. "Wow," he said, realizing he got the best view on the ship too. He wasn't sure if he should just wait in his suite, or go explore the ship. He'd already been around the ship a bit on his first cruise, and he didn't really care to mingle.

Unless Iris was here…

That thought drew him from his room. There were only four rooms on this level, but he couldn't go around banging on doors and demanding to know if she'd booked one of them. They were probably way out of her price range, same as his.

He didn't encounter anyone on his way down to the pool level, and all too soon, the rest of the cruise-goers started boarding the vessel. He still hadn't seen Iris, nor this mystery buddy of his. His hopes started to sink as quickly as he'd thought the last cruise ship was going to, and he turned away from the happy couples, the smiling families.

This was definitely going to be two weeks of torture.

CHAPTER FIFTEEN

*I*ris dashed up the walkway to the cruise ship once more, this time no muscled, tattooed Navy SEAL to help her onto the boat. She made it herself, thanking her foresight for sending Callie down to pretend to be her.

She'd brought her bags, gone through the ruse of arranging to be buddies with Justin Brunner. They'd both been given a suite on the top level of the ship, and while Iris hurried to get through a meeting, Callie had taken care of everything.

All Iris had to do was get to the boat before it left.

And she was once again the last one on the ship. The horn sounded, and the boat moved, and Iris drew in a deep breath. Last time, Justin had hung out near the bar, sipping red and orange smoothies while pretending not to watch her in the pool.

To say the least, she'd been surprised to learn he

was going on the cruise again. She supposed it was for his job, but still. A representative from Cruise Hawaii had offered her a replacement cruise as well, but Iris hadn't called them yet.

But on Friday afternoon, when she'd learned Justin would be on the next cruise out of port, she'd made the call. Booked the ticket. Made last-minute arrangements to be gone for two more weeks.

Now she just needed to find the man and convince him that she didn't blame him, wanted to be with him, and could possibly already be in love with him.

"Have you been on a cruise before?" a man asked, and Iris spun toward him, a powerful sense of déjà vu hitting her square in the chest.

Justin wore a pair of colorful board shorts and a tank top that showed all his glorious muscles and tattoos.

She adjusted her sunglasses, so glad she'd dressed down for the meeting that morning. No more heels. No more pencil skirts. At least not when she was about to spend two incredibly romantic weeks with her boyfriend.

Hopefully, she thought, her fingers trembling the slightest bit.

"Not really," she said, knowing that was how she'd answered last time. "And that is the truth this time." She smiled at him, almost desperate to get the same gesture in return.

"At least you're dressed the part this time." He

scanned her, his eyes taking in every inch of her so very slowly, Iris felt hot from toetip to scalp. "Did you pack that same swimming suit?"

"I threw everything away from last time," she said, taking a step toward him as the boat swayed. She couldn't help the pang of alarm that ran through her, and she scanned to make sure no one else was abandoning ship already. She gave a light laugh when her eyes returned to Justin's. "I'm a little nervous."

"Me too," he admitted, and Iris drew strength from the vulnerability he allowed himself to show to her.

"Justin," she said, deciding to take all the steps toward him. Touch him. Breathe in the scent of his skin. He received her right into his arms, just as he had last time. But he still hadn't smiled, and she still had no idea how he kept all of his emotions behind such a perfectly crafted mask.

"I miss you," she said. "I didn't mean any of those things I said in the hospital. Or before that, on the island. Or anything I might've said in the boat. I was delirious in the boat, so you can't count that against me." She remembered the way he'd commanded those men to get her off the boat and help her, and the memory sparked attraction through her all over again.

She tilted her head back and looked up at him. "You smell like oranges and sunscreen," she said stupidly.

That smile drifted across his lips. Finally. "I don't want to get burnt."

"I thought you were never eating fruit again."

"I'm not," he said. "But I do like drinking it."

"Smoothies."

"They're unlimited on this cruise. Did you know that?"

Iris laughed, the feel of his hands along her waist as magical now as it had been the first time. "I just said that stuff to my family, because my sisters are nosy, nosy Nellies. I didn't want to tell them about you."

"Are you embarrassed of me?" he whispered, his eyes so dark and so dangerous.

"Of course not."

"Then why didn't you want to tell them?"

"Probably the same reason you snuck into my room early in the morning before anyone got there." She gave him a cocked-eyebrow look. "The nurse told me you were there. You came to see me. Why didn't you stay?"

"Probably for the same reason you called me a meathead who made you jump." The bite in his words sank into her soul.

"My reason was because I wasn't sure how you felt about me, and I didn't want to set myself up to get hurt." She had anyway. It had only been a week since Justin had removed himself from her life, but it felt like a lot longer.

"That's my reason too."

"Why wouldn't you let me call you?" she asked.

"Because, Iris." He sighed, the frustration heavy in that sound. "I just…maybe I got my feelings hurt. Just because I act tough and look tough doesn't mean I can't feel."

"I know that."

"Maybe I'd already been doubting us. And feeling bad about hauling you off the boat. And to hear you say that about me…. I just thought maybe we'd had our little tryst and I could get over you."

Iris gazed up at him, so glad he'd been into her enough to have to get over her. "I'm really sorry," she said. "I've been trying to get in touch with you every way I know how since last week. Did Reuben Siddoway tell you I was your client?"

A hint of playfulness entered Justin's eyes, and Iris had her answer.

"I miss you," she repeated. "I'm sorry about what I said and did. That's not how I feel about you." She tipped up on her toes, glad Justin took the bulk of her weight and balanced her. "I don't want to get over you, and I don't want you to get over me. I just want us to be together."

She watched his eyes, though the pull to look at his mouth screamed through her. Seconds stretched between them, and the sun was starting to fry Iris's skin.

"Justin," she said, maybe with the hint of a whine in her voice.

"Oh, are you done?" he asked.

"Yes." She swatted playfully at his chest. "So, what do you think?"

"I think I'm going to kiss you now." He leaned down, wasting no time, and traced his lips across hers. Not really long enough for her to truly experience him. He chuckled, and matched his mouth to hers, finally kissing her like he meant it.

Iris let her pulse accelerate and her fingers trace up the side of his face and into his hair. Kissing him was worth jumping into a lifeboat and only eating dragon fruit for a few days.

Not that she wanted to do it again.

DAYS LATER, SHE AND JUSTIN WERE STILL ON the cruise, no whales in sight. She stuffed herself at every meal, and spent hours by the pool with Justin's hand lazily in hers. They talked about his Navy buddies, and his family, his job. She told him about her sisters, her company, and her desire for a kitten.

By the time they returned to Getaway Bay, Iris had definitely fallen all the way in love with Justin, and he seemed to like her just as much as he had that first time he'd kissed her.

"Hey, so Heath said he'd bring pizza over tonight," Justin said as they disembarked from their cruise. "Do you want to come over and meet him?"

"Sure," Iris said, though she needed a shower with proper water pressure and a chance to get another pedicure. The bottom of the pool had been murder on her toenails. "There's my sister."

Justin glanced at the car where Ivy sat behind the wheel. "She really is your twin," he said.

"Good thing you didn't ask her out through the app before we met." Iris smiled at him, feeling luckier than she had in her whole life.

"Yeah." Justin leaned down and kissed her, a soft, slow union that reminded her of the lazy days they'd shared on the cruise. "See you in a couple of hours." He walked to his truck, and all Iris could do was stare after him.

A sigh leaked from her mouth, just as Ivy joined her on the sidewalk. "You're hopeless."

Iris didn't even try to deny it. "He invited me to meet his friends."

"Ooh, big deal." Ivy heaved Iris's bag into the back seat and went around the front of the car.

"It is a big deal," Iris said. "He has no family here. His crew are his friends and his family." Sudden nerves struck her. What if his friends didn't approve of her?

"I'll have you know that I started dating a guy while you've been gone." Ivy held her chin a couple of inches too high, and Iris pulled herself out of vacation mode. Out of kissing Justin mode, and into twin sister mode.

"You did? Who?"

"He's a great guy," Ivy said, the way she qualified everything. "Brooks Dentin. He's a paralegal for the city."

"Ooh," Iris said, mimicking her sister from a moment ago. "A paralegal. Sounds fancy."

"He's going back to law school."

Iris laughed and ran her hands through her hair. It definitely had too much sunscreen in it still. "I don't care what he does for a living, Ivy."

"Dad does," her twin said very quietly.

Iris swung her attention toward her sister. "Really? He's never said anything to me."

"That's because you're Miss Perfect," Ivy said. "You own your own business. You don't need a man to pay your bills." She looked at Iris, and it was clear she wasn't really upset with her. "But I apparently do."

"Ivy." She reached over and took her sister's hand. "That's not true. Dad doesn't know what he's talking about."

"Maybe not." Ivy shrugged, and Iris didn't know how to erase the hurt in her sister's eyes.

"Let's go get a pedicure," she said. "My treat."

"Really? Do you have time?"

"Of course," Iris said. "I always have time for you, Ivy." That brought a smile to her sister's face, and Iris's spirits lifted. "And you know, I could use some tips on how to meet a guy's family. You do it all the time, but I don't."

"Oh, that's easy," Ivy said with a wave of her hand, her usual bubbly self already back. "Especially this time, because it's going to be all men. You just compliment them. Smile a lot. Touch their arms."

"Ivy," Iris said as she shook her head. "I'm trying to make them like me, not flirt with them."

Ivy looked confused for a moment, which only made Iris laugh harder. "Never mind. I think I can handle it."

She *hoped* she could.

CHAPTER SIXTEEN

Justin had showered, dozed for a bit, and eaten pizza on the couch with Heath, Diego, and Lucas before Iris arrived at his apartment. He practically leapt from the couch, knocking Diego's empty soda can to the floor.

"Whoa, bro," Heath said, looking at him. "Is that her?"

"It's her." Justin wasn't sure why he was so nervous, other than he'd literally never had a woman in his apartment before. Had never introduced a woman to his friends. He looked around at them. "Remember, be honest. If she's like, crazy and I can't see it, tell me."

"She's not going to be crazy," Diego said.

"I don't know," Lucas said, picking up the soda can and stacking it on some dirty plates. "She could be."

That didn't help Justin's nerves as he stepped over

to the door. He opened it and got the best view of his life. Iris leaned into the doorway with her hip cocked, wearing a flirty little sundress in a rainbow of colors.

"Hey," she said, her smile so beautiful and her hair falling in curled waves over both her shoulders.

He wanted to eat her right up. "You know my friends are here, right?" he asked, stepping closer to her and bending his head down to kiss her. He paused an inch from her mouth, sensing her anticipating. "We're not alone."

"I know."

"Why'd you wear this sexy dress, then?" He grinned and touched his mouth to hers. "Because wow, I'd like to be alone with you about now."

She laughed, tipping her head back and exposing her neck. Justin's hormones exploded through him, and he figured he better get her inside so he had an audience. He laced his fingers through hers and tugged her into the apartment. It suddenly smelled like males and marinara—and not in a good way.

"Guys, this is Iris McLaughlin. Iris, these are some of my former SEAL crewmates. Heath, Diego, and Lucas."

She let go of his hand to move around and shake all of theirs. "And you guys are all still active?"

"That's right, ma'am," Heath said, and Justin covered up his laugh with a cough. Heath's bright blue eyes sparkled like the ocean, and Justin decided introducing him to Iris was a very bad idea.

"Justin says you own a landscaping company," Lucas said, handing her a soda.

Iris flicked a glance in his direction. "That's right."

"Pizza?" Diego asked, when not twenty minutes ago he'd refused to get up and get Heath another slice of the supreme.

"Sure," Iris said, sweeping her hair off her shoulder, revealing the tan skin there, with that single strip of pink fabric. Justin wasn't the only one who looked at it. Almost as if all of them had had the same thought, Heath, Diego, and Lucas looked at Justin.

He wasn't getting any weird vibes from them, and he knew Iris was going to be a long-term part of his life when Lucas asked, "Justin also mentioned you having a twin sister. What's her name?"

Heath elbowed him and Diego flat out said, "*I* was going to ask about the sister."

"You snooze, you lose," Lucas said while Diego put a couple of pieces of pizza on a plate and slid it across the island countertop to Iris.

She looked at Justin, a bit of alarm in her eyes. "Guys," he said. "She's not giving you Ivy's number if you act like meatheads."

"*I* have not asked about the sister," Heath said like a dignified English gentleman. "Ivy, you said? She sounds lovely."

Justin started laughing at the same time Iris did, and everything was right in the world. He enjoyed the rest of the evening with his friends and Iris, and finally he got up the nerve to text Heath and ask him to get the guys out of Justin's apartment.

He glanced at his phone, and a moment later said, "Guys, time to go." He got up and started picking up dishes and trash. "We've got an early morning mission to be ready for."

A flash of jealousy stole through him, quickly eradicated when Iris put her hand in his.

"We do?" Diego asked, and Lucas said, "Dude, you never read your texts."

Justin helped get everything cleaned up while Iris curled into herself on the couch. Heath leaned down and kissed her forehead, saying something to her Justin couldn't catch from the kitchen. He left before Justin could catch him, and a moment later his phone chimed.

From Heath: She's perfect for you, you lucky dog.

Justin smiled at the text, at the approval of his friends. "Bye, guys," he called to Lucas and Diego as they said good-bye to Iris too. Finally, the front door closed, and Justin was alone with her again.

"Well," Iris said, getting up from the couch. "They're interesting."

"Interesting good, or interesting bad?" Justin stayed very still while she prowled toward him. "Because we're going to be spending a lot of time with them."

She tiptoed her fingers up his chest. "I liked them a lot, especially Heath."

Relief spread through Justin, along with a healthy

showering of sparks from her touch. He hoped she'd always excite him this much. "I'm glad." He bent down and kissed her, taking his time to let her know how he felt. Words built beneath his tongue, things he'd wanted to say on the cruise but had waited.

"Iris," he whispered, dipping his mouth to taste her neck.

"Hmm?" She held onto him like she couldn't stand without him, and he absolutely loved that. Wanted to take care of her for the rest of his life. Be her man.

"I love you." He looked up and into her eyes just as she opened them.

Surprise flowed freely there, and then she grinned at him, her eyes crinkling around the edges. Joy radiated from her, and Justin smiled too, basking in the warmth of it.

"I love you too, Justin." She kissed him, this time with more passion—and all the love he needed. When she pulled away, she giggled and pressed her face into his chest. "I never thought I'd be grateful for those killer whales who attacked our boat."

She looked up at him again, serious and sweet and oh-so-gorgeous. "But I am."

"Me too," he said, touching the tip of his nose to hers. They might not have every detail worked out yet, but Justin knew they were on the same page about the important things. "Me too."

Read on for a sneak peek at the next book in the series, THE CRUISING FIASCO to see if Orchid can risk her heart and get back into the dating game…

Orchid Stone stapled a packet of papers together, her thoughts on what she should make for dinner that night. She wondered if the other single women in the administration building at Petals & Leis had the same mundane thoughts she did.

She glanced around, though she only worked with three other people. They all looked as bored as she felt, and one of them really needed a boyfriend so they had something to talk about while they filed, answered phones, managed the huge orders that came in, and made sure everyone in the billion-dollar flower company got paid.

But yep, Orchid's life was very, very boring.

She had Tesla, her seven-year-old daughter who kept things hopping, but not during the day while she was at school. And today, Tesla had after-school activities at the recreation center in downtown Getaway Bay, so Orchid wouldn't see her until after dinner, as her father was going to pick Tesla up on his way home from work and take her for something to eat.

Orchid's parents had been lifesavers since the boating accident that had claimed her husband eight years ago.

Eight long years.

She hadn't been on a date since the funeral.

"Jordyn," she said, getting up from her desk. "Didn't you meet someone on that app?"

The pretty brunette rolled her eyes, though Orchid had drawn the interest of the other two women in this part of the building. Cathy and Deirdre both got up and approached Jordyn's desk.

"It was awful," she said with tons of dramatic effect. Jordyn was the youngest in the office, and she'd been the most active on the dating scene. Orchid watched her, a smile on her face, as Jordyn opened a drawer and pulled out a file.

"Total surfer, despite me asking him—twice—if he surfed. And you know how I feel about pretty-boy surfers." She made a face, and Deirdre laughed.

"So he was pretty, then," Orchid said.

"Oh, so pretty." Jordyn smiled. "But I don't want someone who's whole goal in life is to catch the next wave. No. My husband will have ambition. Be someone."

"Sure," Deirdre said. "I'm just hoping for a date."

"There's that new speed-dating thing coming up," Cathy said. "Have you girls heard of it?"

Jordyn shrieked, and Orchid was so glad she'd started this conversation. Anything was better than stapling together vendor packets for the carnation conference next week. Plus, once she finished that, she didn't have a whole lot to do.

Spring was a busy time out in the fields, but in the office, summer and fall and winter were definitely their busiest times.

"Orchid, could I see you a minute?" The voice came from her phone on her desk, and Orchid walked away from the conversation still going strong at Jordyn's desk.

"Yes, Mister Lawson," she said into the intercom. "I'll be right in." She wasn't worried or nervous. Burke Lawson was younger than she was, and while he was set to inherit the entire operation one day, he hadn't done it yet. He did spend a lot of time consulting with his father, and George Lawson did inspire a bit of fear in Orchid.

So when she walked into Burke's office and found his father with him, she stalled. "Oh, hello, George." She closed the door behind her and fought the urge to smooth down her skirt. It suddenly felt too short and like it wasn't good enough as the two of them said hello and shook her hand.

She settled in the chair in front of Burke's desk, and he looked at his father, who nodded.

"Orchid, when's the last time you took a vacation day?"

She blinked, surprise rendering her silent.

"It's been over a year," Burke said for her, flipping open a folder. "You have eighty-four vacation days stockpiled." He closed the folder and smiled.

"I'm—am I in trouble for not taking time off?"

"Yes," he said. "You're a great employee, and we want you to be happy here."

"I am happy here," she said, looking back and forth between them. "Are you firing me?"

"Of course not." He chuckled and pushed the folder toward her. "But take a vacation, Orchid. You work too hard." He stood and smiled her right out of the office, leaving her more confused than ever—and now out of the loop in the conversation at Jordyn's desk.

Later that evening, she stopped by Ivy's apartment rather than facing her house alone. Tesla wouldn't be done with her granddad date for another couple of hours, and Orchid hated entering a dark, empty house by herself.

"There you are," Ivy said, opening the door before Orchid had finished climbing the steps. "What's this about a vacation?"

In response, Orchid practically threw the folder her boss had given her. "This is so stupid."

Ivy took the folder, clear amusement and bewilderment in her eyes, and opened it. A moment later, she sucked in a breath. "Orchid, are you going to do this singles cruise? I've always wanted to go on one of these." She danced in front of Orchid, everything sparkling in her now.

Orchid worked hard not to roll her eyes. "Of course I'm not," she said. "A singles cruise? I can't imagine anything more demeaning. And the fact that my *boss* gave me that pamphlet? *Humiliating.*" She sank onto the couch, wondering where her afternoon had gone. Once she'd gotten the folder and opened it, all she'd been able to do was stare.

Ivy giggled and flipped pages. "They do fun things on these cruises, Orchid. You should totally go."

"Who would watch Tesla?"

"Uh, Mom and Dad," she said. "Eden. Now that she's married, she certainly doesn't need to work. Heaven knows she could take a break from that shed where she's always tinkering."

"I don't want to go on a singles cruise," she said.

"Uh, holy sharks and pearls, Orchid. Did you see this?" She lifted a piece of paper out of the folder.

Orchid had not made it past the first page. "What is that?"

"It's a certificate," she said, her eyes scanning the page. "This cruise is paid for." She exploded to her feet. "Holy shipwrecks, Orchid." Ivy's eyes met Orchid's, and the excitement there was undeniable. "It's. *Paid. For.*"

Orchid couldn't believe it. "That can't be true." She snatched the paper from Ivy, who started hopping around like someone had poured hot ants in her pants. She read the paper too, and sure enough, it certainly looked like she could book a two-week singles cruise free of charge.

"Wow." She lowered the paper, so many emotions battling inside her. "Doesn't mean I have to go."

"Oh, you're going." Ivy took the paper back and pressed it to her chest as if in bliss. Her eyes snapped open. "If you don't want it, can I have it?"

Something about that irked Orchid, and she took the paper and the folder back. "No, Ivy. You're dating Brooks, and he's going to propose any day now. You can't go on a singles cruise."

"I've always wanted to go," she said, a whine in her voice.

"Tell me why," Orchid said, glancing at the closed folder on the couch beside her. She couldn't really go on a singles cruise. Could she?

Ivy started talking about how "super fun" they were, with "all the activities" they planned for people. "It's so much more than laying by the pool," she said. "They have themed cruises, and dances, and trivia, and paint nights." She sighed. "You really should go. I can't believe I haven't suggested this to you before."

Orchid could. She'd made it clear to her sisters that she wasn't interested in dating. Period. The end.

But if she went on a singles cruise, wouldn't that be like dating? Why had her boss given this to her?

Ivy kept talking, as Ivy was wont to do, and Orchid

pulled out her phone and texted Burke. *You gave me a singles cruise? What are you trying to say?*

A singles cruise? His response did not inspire confidence in her. *I don't think so.*

There's a certificate for a singles cruise in that folder you gave me, she typed out, her thumbs moving like lightning over her screen. *What does that mean?*

She hoped she sounded offended and angry, and she must have, because Burke called.

"Yeah?" she answered, not even caring that the word came out like a bark.

"That was an honest mistake," Burke said instead of leading with hello. "I said we should give a few of our hardest working employees a bonus. We looked up who hadn't taken time off in a while, and your name came up. My father said he'd get vacations for each of you, and I didn't think twice about it."

"Who else got one of these?" Orchid asked.

"Leslie in accounting," Burke said, gasping in the next moment. "Lizzie in maintenance. She's married."

Orchid started laughing, and Burke joined in. "I'm sure my father didn't know what he was buying. What's the name of the cruise line?"

"StarMatch," Orchid said, their horrible logo branded on the backs of her eyes.

"It was an innocent mistake," Burke said. "I'll see what I can do about it in the morning. Unless, of course, you want to go on a singles cruise...."

Orchid didn't know what she wanted. She ended up

telling Burke she'd let him know, and she hung up. Turning, she caught Ivy saying, "Yes, of course. Eight a.m. on Thursday. She'll be there."

She hung up the phone too, and when she looked at Orchid, Orchid knew exactly what had just happened.

THURSDAY CAME, AND ORCHID KISSED HER daughter good-bye while Ivy took her suitcase out to the car. She'd tried everything she could to get out of the cruise, but once Ivy had booked it, Burke couldn't get his money back.

"It'll be good for you," Ivy had said in the three days since turning Orchid's life upside down.

"You need this." That was another one her sister had said several times.

Even Eden and Iris had gotten behind the idea of a singles cruise. Eden had come over last night and packed a backpack for Orchid with all the emergency supplies she'd need. She'd hugged her sister and told her to have fun.

Iris had sent her a list of ways to flirt with a winky face, and Orchid had been mortified. Her sisters knew what she'd been through. They knew she hadn't dated in eight long years. They knew her better than anyone.

And that alone was what had her boarding the ship along with twenty-six other thirty-and-flirty-some-things, her flip flops pinching between her toes.

Orchid had a hard time determining age when she looked at the men and women already onboard. She certainly felt older than all of them, and she wondered if any of them had children. Had been married before. Had buried a spouse.

Her emotions spiraled, but she put on a smile, the way Ivy had told her to. She turned toward the closest man, determined to talk to him. That way, when Ivy messaged her and asked her how things were going, Orchid could say she'd at least tried.

Maybe that was all she needed to do. Try.

"Hey," she said to the impossibly tall man in front of her. His brown hair seemed like it needed a cut, but the shaggy locks looked good on him. He wore a full beard too, and Orchid tried not to swoon.

So maybe this would be good for her.

"My name's Orchid," she said, finally drawing the man's attention to her.

He didn't smile. Didn't even act like he heard her. Maybe he hadn't. He was quite a bit taller than her. Wider.

Another blonde joined them, creating a little triangle. She also wore little triangles of fabric over her private parts—and not much else. "Hey," she said. "I'm Amber."

"Maine," the man said, and it seemed like every female on the ship flocked toward him then.

Orchid took a step back, disgusted by him. He couldn't even acknowledge that she'd spoken to him?

Sure, maybe she wasn't as pretty and perky as Amber, but she had a cute swimming suit on too—underneath her clothes.

"Jerk," she muttered, deciding to get out of the sun for a little bit. She didn't have to tell Ivy she'd only tried one conversation.

She'd tried.

As she locked herself in her room, she couldn't help feeling like this singles cruise was a bad, bad idea.

Oooh, Orchid put herself out there and was shot down! What's with that Maine guy? ;)

Read THE CRUISING FIASCO in ebook or paperback!

The Perfect Storm (Book 1): A freak storm has her sliding down the mountain...right into the arms of her ex. As Eden and Holden spend time out in the wilds of Hawaii trying to survive, their old flame is rekindled. But with secrets and old feelings in the way, will Holden be able to take all the broken pieces of his life and put them back together in a way that makes sense? Or will he lose his heart and the reputation of his company because of a single landslide?

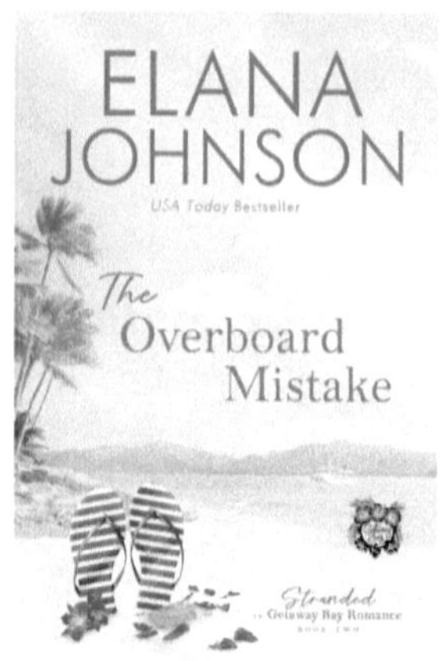

The Overboard Mistake (Book 2): Friends who ditch her. A pod of killer whales. A limping cruise ship. All reasons Iris finds herself stranded on an deserted island with the handsome Navy SEAL...

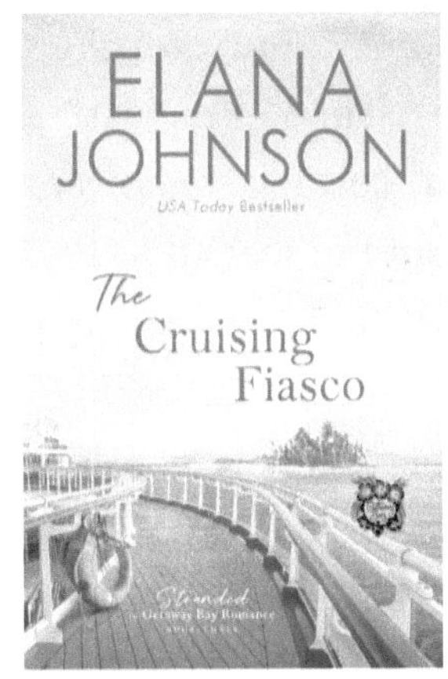

The Cruising Fiasco (Book 3): He can throw a precision pass, but he's dead in the water in matters of the heart...

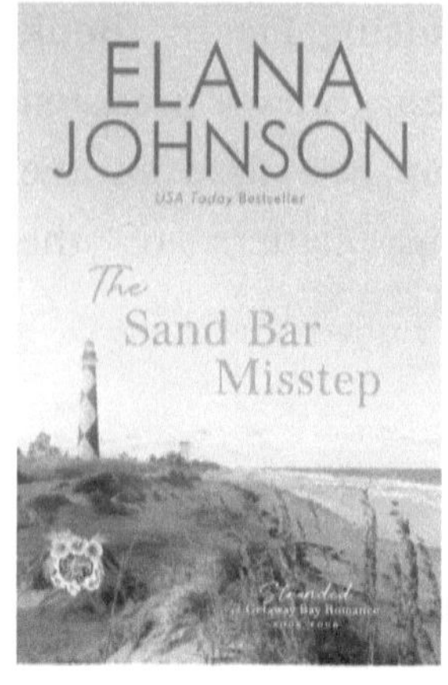

The Sand Bar Misstep (Book 4): Tired of the dating scene, a cowboy billionaire puts up an Internet ad to find a woman to come out to a deserted island with him to see if they can make a love connection...

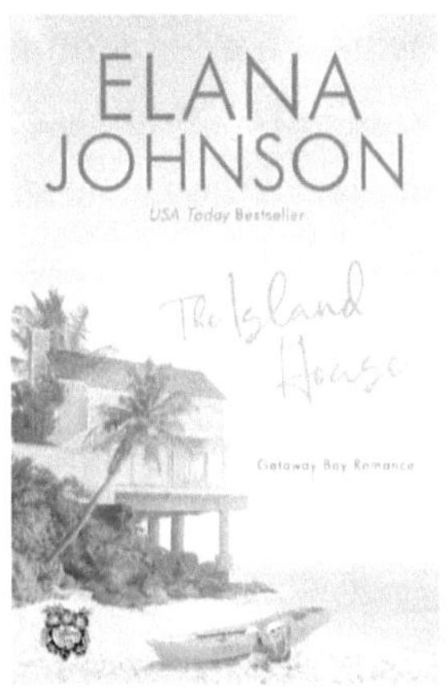

The Island House (Book 1): Charlotte Madsen's whole world came crashing down six months ago with the words, "I met someone else."

Can Charlotte navigate the healing process to find love again?

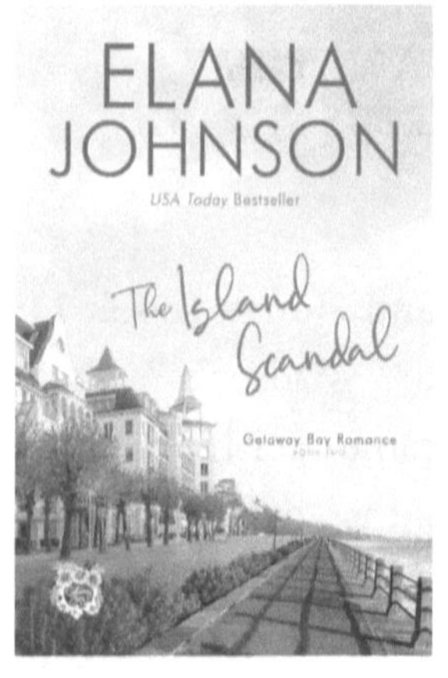

The Island Scandal (Book 2): Ashley Fox has known three things since age twelve: she was an excellent seamstress, what her wedding would look like, and that she'd never leave the island of Getaway Bay. Now, at age 35, she's been right about two of them, at least.

Can Burke and Ash find a way to navigate a romance when they've only ever been friends?

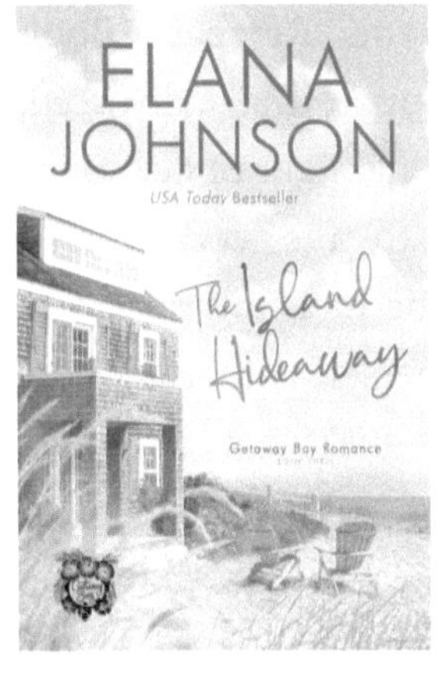

The Island Hideaway (Book 3): She's 37, single (except for the cat), and a synchronized swimmer looking to make some extra cash. Pathetic, right? She thinks so, and she's going to spend this summer housesitting a cliffside hideaway and coming up with a plan to turn her life around.

Can Noah and Zara fight their feelings for each other as easily as they trade jabs? Or will this summer shape up to be the one that provides the romance they've each always wanted?

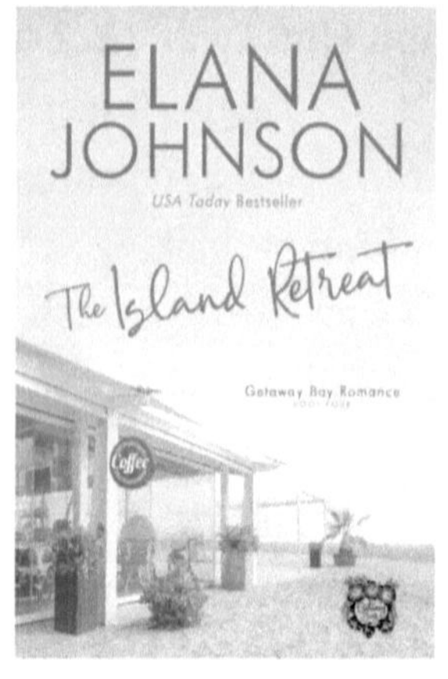

The Island Retreat (Book 4): Shannon's 35, divorced, and the highlight of her day is getting to the coffee shop before the morning rush. She tells herself that's fine, because she's got two cats and a past filled with emotional abuse. But she might be ready to heal so she can retreat into the arms of a man she's known for years...

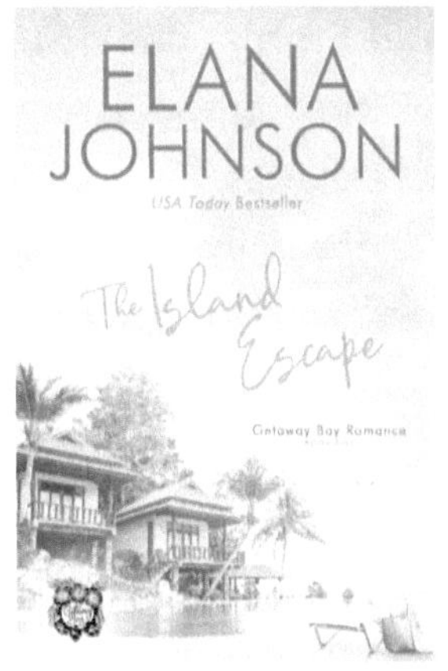 **The Island Escape (Book 5):** Riley Randall has spent eight years smiling at new brides, being excited for her friends as they find Mr. Right, and dating by a strict set of rules that she never breaks. But she might have to consider bending those rules ever so slightly if she wants an escape from the island...

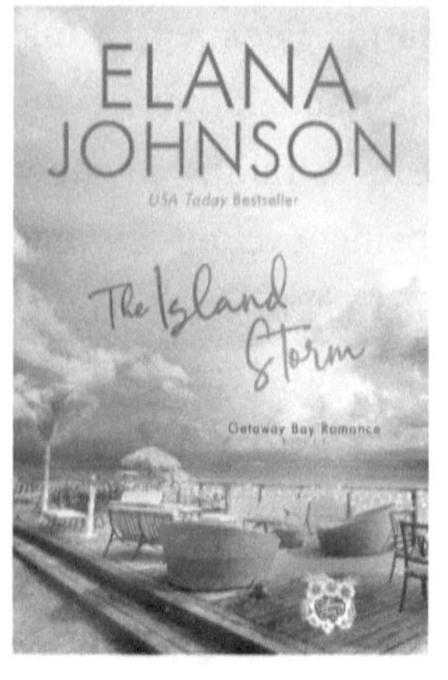

The Island Storm (Book 6): Lisa is 36, tired of the dating scene in Getaway Bay, and practically the only wedding planner at her company that hasn't found her own happy-ever-after. She's tried dating apps and blind dates...but could the company party put a man she's known for years into the spotlight?

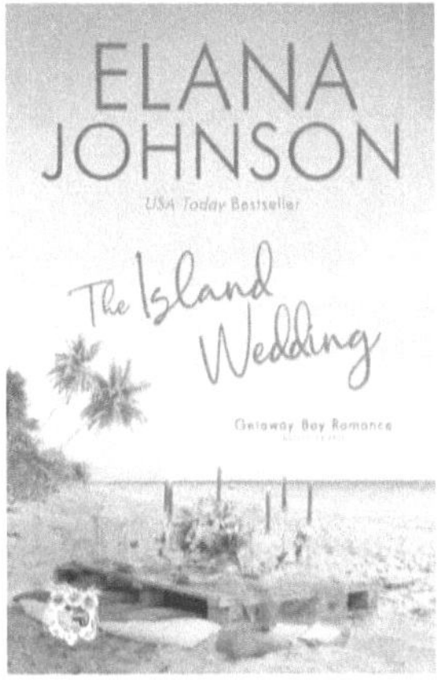

The Island Wedding (Book 7): Deirdre is almost 40, estranged from her teenaged daughter, and determined not to feel sorry for herself. She does the best she can with the cards life has dealt her and she's dreaming of another island wedding...but it certainly can't happen with the widowed Chief of Police.

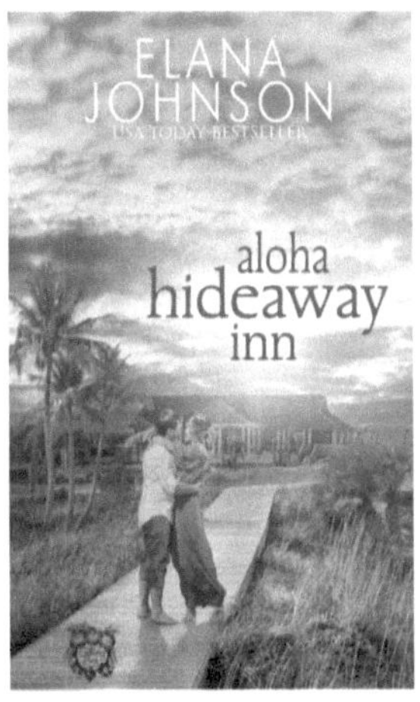

Aloha Hideaway Inn (Book 1): Can Stacey and the Aloha Hideaway Inn survive strange summer weather, the arrival of the new resort, *and* the start of a special relationship?

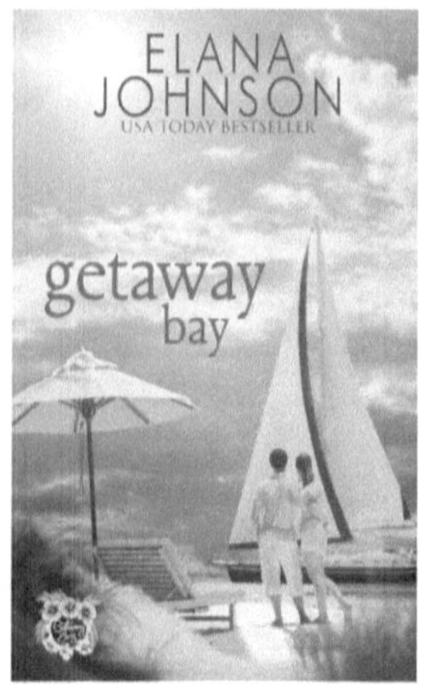

Getaway Bay (Book 2): Can Esther deal with dozens of business tasks, unhappy tourists, *and* the twists and turns in her new relationship?

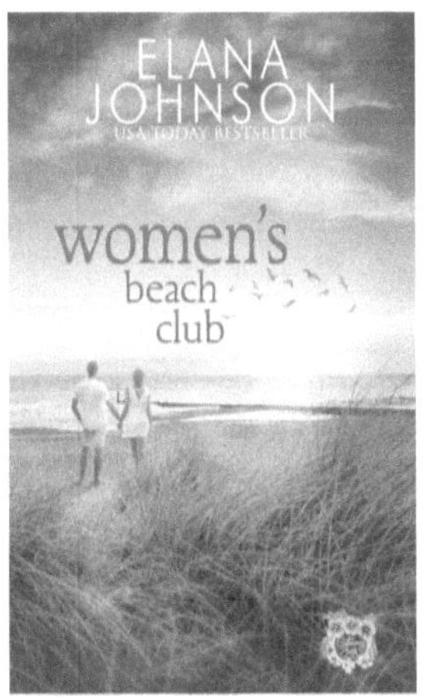

Women's Beach Club (Book 3): With the help of her friends in the Beach Club, can Tawny solve the mystery, stay safe, and keep her man?

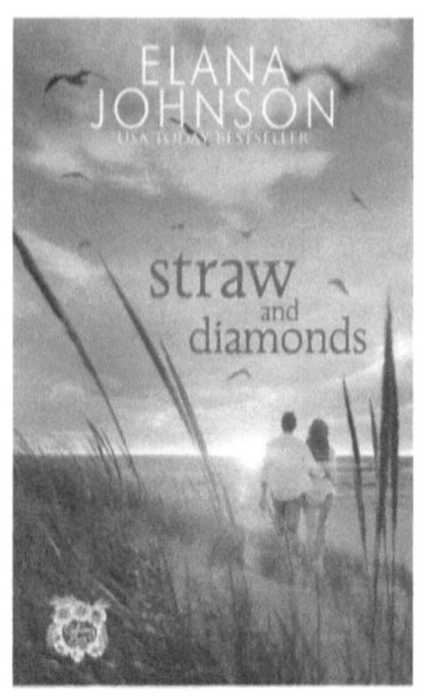

Straw and Diamonds (Book 4): Can Sasha maintain her sanity amidst their busy schedules, her issues with men like Jasper, and her desires to take her business to the next level?

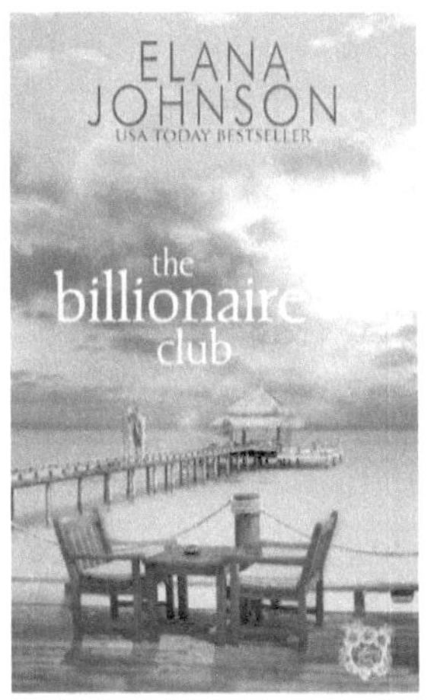

The Billionaire Club (Book 5): Can Lexie keep her business affairs in the shadows while she brings her relationship out of them? Or will she have to confess everything to her new friends...and Jason?

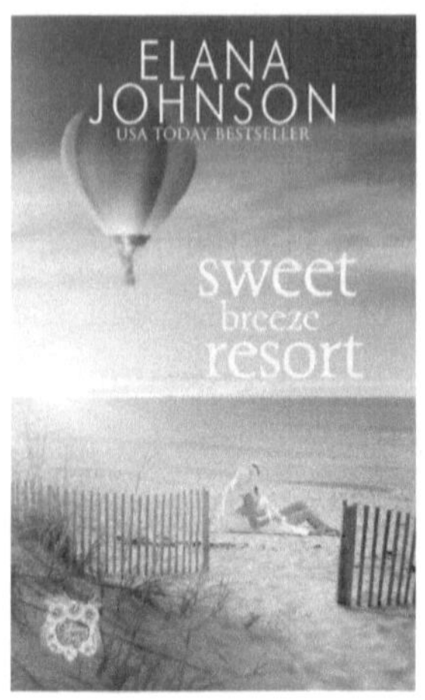

Sweet Breeze Resort (Book 6): Can Gina manage her business across the sea and finish the remodel at Sweet Breeze, all while developing a meaningful relationship with Owen and his sons?

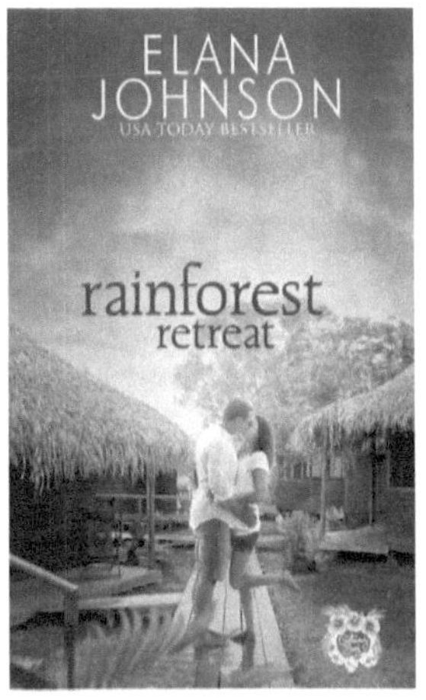

Rainforest Retreat (Book 7): As their paths continue to cross and Lawrence and Maizee spend more and more time together, will he find in her a retreat from all the family pressure? Can Maizee manage her relationship with her boss, or will she once again put her heart—and her job—on the line?

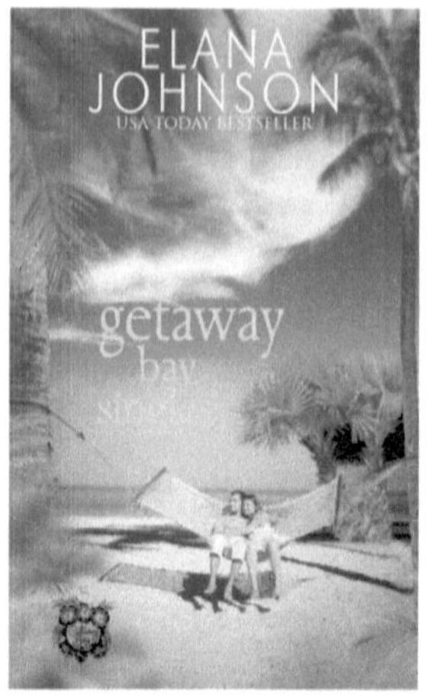

Getaway Bay Singles (Book 8): Can Katie bring him into her life, her daughter's life, and manage her business while he manages the app? Or will everything fall apart for a second time?

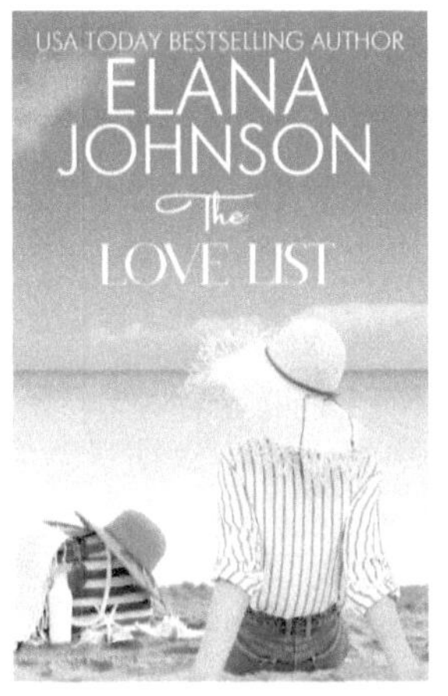

The Love List (Hilton Head Romance, Book 1): Bea turns to her lists when things get confusing and her love list morphs once again... Can she add *fall in love at age 45* to the list and check it off?

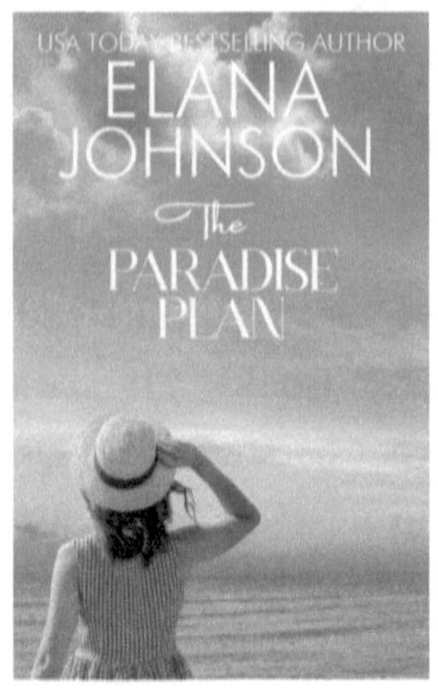

The Paradise Plan (Hilton Head Romance, Book 2): When Harrison keeps showing up unannounced at her construction site, sometimes with her favorite pastries, Cass starts to wonder if she should add him to her daily routine... If she does, will her perfectly laid out plans fall short of paradise? Or could she find her new life *and* a new love, all without any plans at all?

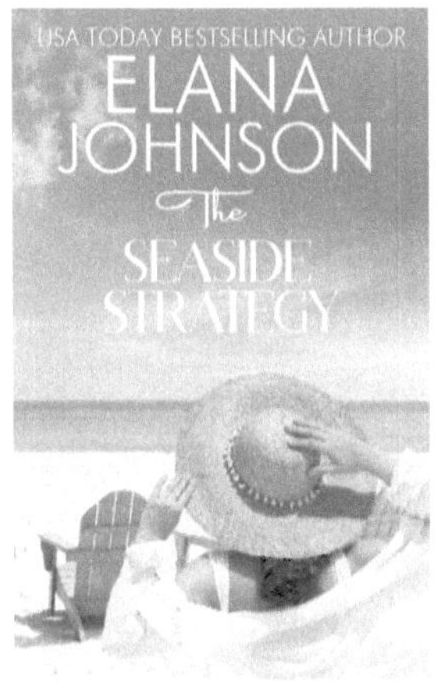

The Seaside Strategy (Hilton Head Romance, Book 3): Lauren doesn't want to work for Blake, especially not in strategic investments. She's had enough of the high-profile, corporate life. **Can she strategically insert herself into Blake's life without compromising her** seaside strategy and finally get what she really wants...love and a lasting relationship?

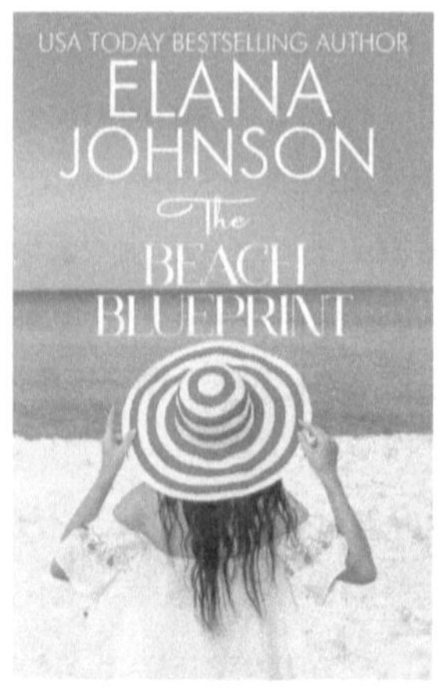

The Beach Blueprint (Hilton Head Romance, Book 4): Joy Bartlett needs a blueprint before she takes a single step in any direction. She loves seeing what she's getting into before committing, and moving 1200 miles from Texas to South Carolina just because half of her Supper Club has doesn't mean she's going to start packing boxes. Can she figure out how to arrange all of the pieces in her life in a way that makes sense? Or will she find herself cut off from everyone who's ever been important to her?

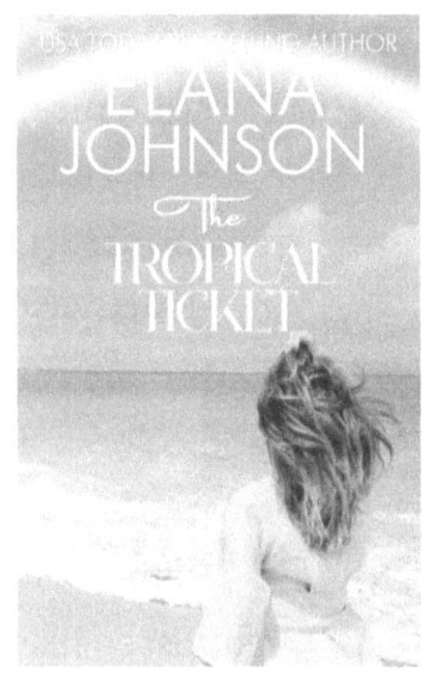

The Tropical Ticket (Hilton Head Romance, Book 5): Bessie Clifton adores baking. With her daughter Wynona by her side, she's turned her passion for the perfect loaf of bread into a dream for a bakery. They move to Hilton Head Island and work to get their shop open with the help of Bessie's five best friends.

It's not just a relocation.

It's a reinvention.

Will Bessie's journey to self-discovery lead her to the love she's always craved?

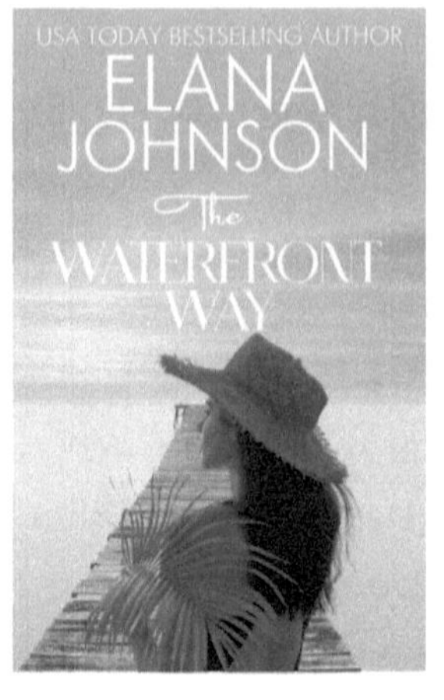

The Waterfront Way (Hilton Head Romance, Book 6): Sage Grady is a master of transformation. She's a seasoned hairstylist who's perfected the art of change, one cut and color at a time. Yet, her own life has started to feel somewhat monotonous, almost like she's stuck in someone else's style–and she needs to shake things up.

It's not a mid-life crisis.

It's a new way of thinking, of living.

Will she find that the path to true love doesn't always follow the path most trod, but might just be discovered through...the waterfront way?

Elana Johnson is the USA Today bestselling and Kindle All-Star author of dozens of clean and wholesome contemporary romance novels. She lives in Utah, where she mothers two fur babies, works with her husband full-time, and eats a lot of veggies while writing. Find her on her website at feelgoodfictionbooks.com

www.ingramcontent.com/pod-product-compliance
Lightning Source LLC
Chambersburg PA
CBHW021959130726
47903CB00014B/2490